Christian Carnal Cravings

Also by Tyler

Castle Bleu, The Beginning

Christian Carnal Cravings 2:
The Saga Continues
Available Summer 2015

Tribulations of the Brothers Black.
(Lancelot Valiant and Jeffery Carter)
Available Summer 2015

Hunter, Slayer of Covens
Available Summer 2015

Christian Carnal Cravings

Tyler

The Butterfly Typeface Publishing
Little Rock Arkansas

For additional information you may address
The Butterfly Typeface Publisher, PO Box 56193, Little Rock Arkansas 72215.

First Edition

ISBN 978-1-942022-09-1

Forgive me for being merely a foolish woman
Often questioning both HIS purpose
and HIS unchanging Plan
I know HE's there, calling me,
but you must understand
I'm no machine, despite what they say,
I feel, like any human

Tyler

Acknowledgments

SEVERAL people have motivated and inspired me in their own ways for which I am extremely thankful, but only a few can be mentioned. I am thankful for my family and would like them to know that I love them dearly!

I would like to thank my mother, Oara, for her love, generosity and encouragement, my son, who has wisdom beyond his years and has always been God's voice in my life ever since he could speak, My Dearest friend, Ellen, for encouraging me when everything around me seemed to be falling apart at the seams, Iris, who inspired, encouraged and motivated me to write this story, and of course God who gave me the talent and words but should receive all the Glory.

Sin

IT WAS Sunday morning and as usual, she went to church. She sat there silently, focused, but not on the preacher. She was a million miles away. Her thoughts still lingered on the night before …

She had been invited to attend a birthday party for her sister. She didn't know why she had decided against her better judgment to attend, but she felt obligated to do so. She hadn't been to a nightclub in years. Her new life had fulfilled her completely, at first, but as of late, she began to lose the excitement she once felt with being a Christian. She wasn't thinking of turning her back on God, not ever, but she was physically alone and she did not enjoy it. She had no husband or children. No one to come home to except her pet cat, who was independent as well.

When she got the phone call from Frances, she shook her head as if she could actually see her.

"Frances, you know I don't go to nightclubs. Why are you even asking me to attend such a thing?" She replied as she fought her smile. The thought of being in a nightclub with all the loud music and dancing began to creep its way into her mind in spite of her efforts to block the desires.

"C'mon Rae, it will be fun. I promise if you don't have a good time, I won't ask you to go out again. Not even on my birthday. C'mon it will be fun! You don't have to drink if you don't want. You can have soda or water. I'll make sure you don't get drunk and embarrass me because that's exactly what I plan to do. I am going to get loaded! So, I won't have time to be embarrassed about what you do. Ha ha!"

"Very nice Frances. You really want me to go? I think you are trying to talk me out of it. I don't want to see you get loaded that will definitely be embarrassing. Can't you think of another way to celebrate your birthday?"

"I didn't think of this one. Some of the girls from the office thought it up. I'm going along because I'm the birthday girl. Geez! Loosen up Rae. Live a little bit. It won't kill you to go out with me one night of the year! You can get back to your locked up room of a world tomorrow. What do you say?"

"Frances, you are truly amazing. I can't believe I even call you a friend let alone a sister. You never ask me to do anything I don't want to do at all. You are the most considerate person I've ever met. I'm being sarcastic in case you were too busy flattering yourself to notice my tone of voice."

"Hey, no one is twisting your arm. It's okay. Forget I even asked. I just thought you might want to go and help me celebrate my birthday. If it's too much for you to make me happy, then never mind."

With those words, Frances hung up the phone.

Rachel hadn't meant to disappoint her sister, so she sighed deeply, looked at the telephone still in her hand, and then quickly decided to call her back, just as Frances knew she would. She answered so quickly, Rachel knew she had done exactly what Frances had expected her to do.

"Hello, Rachel. That took you a long time." Frances was trying to conceal her giggle, but Rachel knew she had been tricked.

"Why you....." Rachel thought, but instead of vocalizing her irritation, she took another deep breath before speaking.

"Alright Frances, you've managed to make me feel stupid again. Tell me where it will be and all the other information I need to get there."

"I knew I could count on you, Rachel! You are the best sister anyone could ever ask for! You'll have a great time. I'll make sure you do. The name of the club is "Optical Illusions" and it's right on the outskirts of the downtown area. 216 Woonsocket Boulevard. It's a huge place. You can't miss it. If you do, give me a call and I'll find you. Just tell the door attendant that you are a part of the Jensen Birthday party and they will let you in."

"I'm the best sister? I'm your only sister. I think you only like me when I give in to your craziness. When I ask you to go to church with me, you don't want to talk, but that's all right Frances. I'll be there, but I won't stay long. I'm just coming to let your friends know that you do have a sister, but after that, I'm leaving."

"Thank you Rachel. You won't be sorry. I wouldn't ask you to do anything more than meet my friends, you are the best!"

The loud applause echoed throughout the church snatching her from her thoughts abruptly.

"Amen! Amen!" The congregation shouted.

She lifted her hands as she looked around slowly and clapped instinctively, but soon drifted back into last night at the club.

Against her better judgment, she had decided she would attend the birthday party for her sister even though she told herself that Frances had tricked her into it.

"Frances. What am I going to do with you?" She thought as she rummaged through her closet for something to wear to the party.

Rachel decided to wear a modest dress that touched her knees. The dress was a soft orchid colored short-sleeved dress, with a scoop neckline and a flare tail that reminded her of dancer's dress. She laughed to herself at that thought because she knew she would not be doing any dancing. She stood in front of her mirror as she pushed her hair away from her face and wrapped it into a long ponytail.

She didn't want to overdo her appearance, but she didn't want Frances to be ashamed of her. She decided that what she wore was perfect, nothing fancy and nothing drab.

Once she was satisfied with what she wore, she made her way to her car and drove carefully to the location of the nightclub.

Rachel didn't mind driving alone at night, but she rarely did it because she had to get to work early the next day usually. She did during emergencies such as low food supplies, forgotten gifts and if Frances needed her.

"I'll go inside, say hello to everyone then I'll leave. It's as simple as that, no more, no less."

She told herself repeatedly as she approached the brightly light entrance. She blinked as her eyes adjusted to the glare but continued to walk closer to the entrance. The door attendant stared at her as she approached then, he smiled brightly as she spoke.

He was tall and slender with dark hair and very pale grayish blue eyes. Rachel couldn't help but smile at him and felt silly about it until he smiled back at her which caused her to blush. "Oh my." She thought as she stood there trying to remain calm in front of him. Her body began to tremble instinctively and she wrapped her arms across her chest as if she were cold. She looked away for a moment, then turned back to him smiling politely.

He wore the club uniform, a long sleeved white dress shirt, black slacks and a black vest with the name of the club, Optical Illusions, stitched on the upper left side.

Rachel began to feel what she thought was embarrassed and wanted to get to Frances as quickly as possible so she could go home.

"I'm here for the Frances Jensen Birthday party. Can you tell me where it is?"

"I certainly can. I just need to make sure your name is on the guest list. Do you have an ID?"

"Yes, here it is." She said as she handed him her driver's license.

"Very Good, Ms. Jensen, or would you prefer I call you Rachel?" He winked as he spoke to her. She fought the urge to giggle.

"I, uh…Rachel is fine thank you."

"I definitely agree with you there," He replied, pausing momentarily to look at her then smiled before continuing.

 "Rachel is definitely, fine. In fact, I'd say she's absolutely gorgeous, but that may be considered as harassment, wouldn't it?" His voice was like a gentle symphony in her ears, causing her to blush followed by a barely audible sigh as he bowed his head slightly, then gestured for her to follow him deeper into the club. The blaring music drowned out all other sounds. Rachel was surprised by this club.

Everything seemed fast paced. People were dancing close together, but appeared to be doing more than just dancing. Rachel's eyes grew wide as she watched. She was both curious and appalled at the same time.

The door attendant saw the look on her face as she watched the dancers. He beckoned to her as her eyes found him in the crowd.

"Oh!"

Rachel fought the urge to cover her ears as she followed the door attendant through the tightly packed crowd. People were screaming, cheering, dancing, laughing and drinking all around her. There was barely any room to walk inside the club. She felt bodies closing in on her as she cautiously looked around. She was very uncomfortable in this setting. She had not been in a nightclub since she had graduated from high school almost six years ago.

She tried not to notice as several men smiled at her from every angle. Some smiles were polite, others were clearly very wicked making her feel as if they were slowly removing her clothes from her body in their minds. She stared wide eyed as if she could read their minds, then quickly turned to find the door attendant who walked through the crowd easily, but looked back occasionally for her. He noticed that she was struggling with getting through the crowd and stopped to wait for her. He had forgotten that he was an expert at maneuvering his way through the crowd whereas most other people were not. He stood silently and patiently as he waited for her to catch up to him.

When she caught up to him, she stopped, looked at him, and then took a deep breath. She felt as if she had been running around in circles for half an hour without rest. Her mind was clouding up as the music continued to pound in her ears. She squinted and looked around for Frances, or someone familiar.

"You okay?" he asked politely.

"Yes, I'm fine. How much farther?" she asked

"This is the table right here." He replied

Rachel looked around, but did not see anyone she recognized.

"Are you sure? This is the Jensen party table?" She managed to screech above the blaring music.

"Yes, I'm sure. I've had to lead a couple of ladies this way. Maybe they are dancing, or they are in the back with the dancers. I'll lead you there. Follow me please, Rachel." He said instinctively reaching for her hand, but she pulled away. He looked at her for a moment, then smiled politely.

"It's okay. I'm not going to hurt you. I just didn't want to lose track of you. People are packed like sardines in here tonight. Forgive me if I was being too forward. I didn't mean any disrespect."

He turned and began to slowly walk through the crowd again. Rachel believing that she had hurt the door attendant's feelings caught up to him and took hold of his hand.

"What's the big deal? I'm not dating anyone and this isn't anything bad....right?" She thought to herself as he smiled at her.

"I'm sorry. I should not have been so rude. I hope I didn't offend you." She said to the door attendant.

"Not at all, I was way out of line, but I'm glad that you've forgiven me. Thank you, Rachel." The door attendant said. Rachel couldn't help herself now and began to blush.

The door attendant smiled at her, tilted his head toward her and whispered into her ear.

"Please call me Sean. I don't remember introducing myself to you before, but I hope you will remember me, not just tonight, but any night."

He was close enough to her ear to brush his lips gently across it. She shivered slightly from the closeness, but found it to be enticing. She smiled at him as he straightened his body, still staring at her.

"That's a nice name. I am sure I will remember it, Sean." Rachel replied smiling.

Sean winked at her then held her hand tightly, leading her through the crowd until they reached an area that was not so populated. The lights were dim and the music that played in this section was much more seductive. Rachel looked around slowly taking it all in.

"This place is huge. It doesn't look so big from the outside, but inside, it's really quite amazing!" she said softly. Sean turned to her smiling seductively as he spoke.

"Who, me? You haven't seen nothing yet, Rachel. I'd really love to show you everything though."

Rachel stared at him as if he were speaking another language. He led her to a darkened corner, then snatched her into his arms. She gasped in surprise as he kissed her neck and maneuvered her pressing her back against the wall gently. He wasn't rough with her, but his actions told her that he wanted her. She wanted to push away from him and scream, but to her surprise, her body did not obey her mind's commands.

"You don't remember me at all, do you Rachel? That's okay, I could never forget you!"

Her thoughts were going wild as he pressed his body against hers. She breathed deeply as her body began to relax in his embrace. She was lonely and wanted to be physically loved, but how much did she know about this man? She couldn't allow herself to be taken like this so easily, but her body wasn't willing to fight his hold on her. She found herself succumbing to his touch and complying with his desires.

He slowly slid his hand into her panties as he continued to kiss her. She instantly squeezed his wrist wanting mentally to stop him from touching her so intimately, but then she relaxed her grip upon him allowing him further access to her. She gasped softly, trembling slightly as he touched her. She bit her lip and breathed deeply, but did not reject his continued exploration of her.

"Mmmm!" The sound barely escaped from beneath the pressure of his hungry lips against hers.

They breathed hard rapid breaths between their intense kisses. She felt weakened and closed her eyes slowly. She didn't want to think about the consequences, she simply wanted to enjoy the moment. Suddenly, she heard Frances' voice.

"I wonder where Rachel could be. I thought she said she would come, but she hasn't made it here yet? Maybe she changed her mind again. She's such an old lady." Frances laughed with her friends as they made their way past the barely secluded wall where Rachel and Sean were making out.

Rachel felt like an idiot and gently nudged away from Sean. He wanted to comfort her, but he didn't know exactly how.

"Rachel..." he began but she cut him off.

"Its fine, but I really should go now. Goodbye Sean." She said as she rushed off into the crowd searching for the exit. She needed to get as far away from him as possible and took advantage of the present opportunity, fleeing the scene as quickly as she could.

Frances had always been the wild one of the family. She was always so open and promiscuous. She didn't mind sharing intimate details with Rachel about the men she dated. Rachel was much more reserved. She focused on school mostly. She had an occasional boyfriend here and there, but never anything as wild as Frances had. Rachel was not a virgin. She had one relationship that became serious before, but it was over when she graduated from college.

When they were in college, Frances was always attending parties while Rachel studied for finals. Frances had undergone abortions twice as far as Rachel knew and naturally did not approve.

Rachel rushed to her car and drove home.

She wasn't upset about what Frances said about her. She knew her sister thought of her in that way, but she was upset from what almost happened with Sean. She barely even knew him, but she had allowed herself to submit to him sexually. She felt ashamed of herself as she looked in the mirror. She couldn't stop her tears from falling.

"What have I done? God forgive me, please!" she collapsed upon her bed and began to cry.

She was so alone and so aroused she could not think straight at all. She wished she hadn't left the nightclub, but she was glad she had. She was conflicted emotionally. She didn't realize that she was touching herself at first, but when she did realize it, she didn't want to stop. She closed her eyes and parted her legs, pretending that Sean was there, touching her. She breathed hard as her fingers slid along her moistened sensitive folds. She shut her eyes tightly as her breathing intensified with her body's quivers, bit her lip to silence her growing pleasure, then as suddenly as the tremors began, they ended. She breathed slowly and deeply, relaxing her once anxious body against her bed. She stared up at the ceiling and blinked slowly as tears gradually fell.

"Am I a bad person for feeling like this? What is wrong with me?"

The loud praise of the congregation yanked her out of her thoughts so rapidly, she had forgotten where she was. She looked around quickly taking in the view and breathed deeply.

She had to stay focused on the service. She looked at the preacher as he continued his sermon. He wasn't the average preacher. Reverend Andrew was rather young and handsome in his dark suit. Rachel smiled then shook her head as if trying to focus on what he was saying and erasing all other thoughts regarding the reverend.

"I say to you repent! Turn from your evil ways for the day and hour is at hand! We have to be ready for his glorious return! Will you be ready?" he shouted to the congregation as they all cheered and applauded.

Rachel felt as if she had been slapped in the face as the preacher continued to rouse the congregation with his words. They cheered loudly, lifting their hands high into the air as she sank into her seat. She wished she could crawl beneath the chair and disappear completely. She looked around at the congregation slowly. Everyone was on their feet ....except Cheryl.

Cheryl was the preacher's wife and a very prominent figure in the church. She organized women's ministry groups and taught Sunday school lessons occasionally. She and her husband had organized church meetings, outings and visits to other churches together. They had been married for five years and the entire congregation thought of them as a model couple.

Rachel looked around at the congregation silently, clapping her hands, then spotted Cheryl. The two of them stared at each other for a moment cautiously, then Rachel quickly turned away. She had hoped she didn't aroused any suspicions in Cheryl's mind. She closed her eyes, feeling even more ashamed of herself and began to talk to herself mentally.

"God's love should be enough for me. Why am I feeling so sleazy? Nothing happened....well..." she tried to comfort herself in her head.

She lowered her head attempting to shield herself from the shame she felt in silence as the congregation continued to shout all around her. She struggled with her feelings in silence and fought against her tears.

"I should never have gone there, ever. I should know better than letting her talk me into such things."

She attempted to blame Frances, Sean and everyone else she could think of for her visit to the nightclub, but she knew deep down inside that none of them were to blame. She was simply trying to justify her own actions. She used Frances' request as a scapegoat to what SHE had really wanted for herself.

She sat quietly blinking hard in the middle of the roaring applause of the congregation.

When the service was over, the congregation began their ritual of shaking hands and hugging each other while participating in small talk. This was to show solidarity in the spirit of the church. A few members smiled at her causing her to nod and smile politely back.

Rachel already felt like an outcast. She felt as if she were so unclean from what happened with Sean that her sin cloaked her and the other members could feel it. No one truly holy wanted to be near someone they knew to be such a blatant sinner. Rachel blinked rapidly to stop the onset of developing tears, lifted her head and tried to put on a brave face as she slowly made her way toward the door of the church.

Rachel smiled weakly as the other members walked around and shook hands with each other having brief polite conversations before making their way back to their own lives. Cheryl eventually reached Rachel and extended her hand to her.

"Rachel, God bless you honey. How are you feeling today?" Cheryl asked as she extended her hand and took hold of Rachel's.

"I'm fine, thank you Mrs. Cheryl." Rachel responded weakly. She could barely hear herself speak. She looked around as if she were trying to spot the nearest exit.

 "Oh no, she knows! She knows what happened! But how could she? She wasn't there. She knows I didn't do right! Oh no! She's going to tell everyone and they will all label me as a tramp! It was an honest mistake. Who am I trying to kid? They all know about it. Mrs. Cheryl is the only one who is nice enough to try to talk to me. She is the wife of the Reverend after all. It's their job to assist the lost souls and other sinners."

She began to shiver as Cheryl continued to talk to her. She blocked Cheryl's words mentally and continued to look around the church. She wanted to leave before her guilt became too much for her to bear. She looked down at her shoes, then at the walls as Cheryl continued speaking.

Then Cheryl stopped suddenly. She stared at Rachel for a moment who clearly couldn't tell that she was no longer speaking. Rachel looked at her shoes again, turning her feet to the side trying to decide if she should wear them to work the next day or wear another pair instead. Cheryl raised a curious eyebrow at Rachel and brought her back to the present when she addressed her.

"Rachel? Girl, where is your mind today? You were practically dozing during the service. I saw you." Cheryl asked.

Rachel quickly looked at her and her eyes grew wide with terror at Cheryl's words. "I saw you."

Rachel breathed short rapid breaths as panic began to overtake her. She had to leave immediately.

"I'm sorry. I was supposed to meet my sister today. Yesterday was her birthday and I wanted to do something nice for her. Please excuse me, Mrs. Cheryl. It's been nice talking to you."

"Mmmhmm. I was really talking to myself, Rachel. You know you should bring that sister of yours here and try to save her lost soul. My husband is good at telling people that God will save them."

Cheryl sighed deeply as she spoke her last words. Rachel looked at her.

"She almost sounds sarcastic." Rachel thought.

Cheryl turned her head slowly and spotted her husband talking with some other members of the church. Then she rolled her eyes slightly away from him as if disappointed and returned her eyes to Rachel who tried not to stare at her in obvious surprise. Cheryl smiled politely as Rachel remained silent in spite of her failed attempts to shield her surprise. She gently pat Rachel's hand as she began to speak to her again.

"It's just a thought. No one will be angry if you can't talk her into coming. I'm not trying to twist your arm and make you do something you don't want to do either. It's all up to you, of course, but if you can get her to come, we will definitely be glad to have her here." Cheryl smiled politely as she quickly flung her arms around Rachel's shoulders, embracing her tightly.

"Whatever is bothering you, Rachel, God will take care of it. He will give you the peace you are in search of." Cheryl whispered into Rachel's ear before she released her and immediately walked over to another church member. They embraced quickly and began to talk.

Rachel couldn't stand it any longer and quickly made her way to the parking lot. She practically ran to her car and drove home.

Betrayal

WHEN SHE walked into her apartment, she heard her telephone ringing. She placed her keys on the table next to the door and picked up the receiver. She didn't really feel like talking to anyone, but she thought it best to answer.

"Hello?" She said as politely as she could muster up.

"Rae! What happened to you last night? I told the girls that you were coming. Do you have any idea how stupid you made me look? Wow! You! You lied to me! I can't believe that you lied to me! Did you even attempt to show or did you just *plan* to make me look stupid? Unbelievable! This is unforgivable Rae! I'm not speaking to you anymore! You could have just said you didn't want to come and not lead me to think that you were going to actually show! UGH!"

"I did show! I was..." Rachel covered her mouth quickly as if blocking the words from escaping her lips.

The last thing she wanted to do was to tell Frances about her make out session with Sean. She pressed her lips together further stopping them from moving. She had to think about what she wanted to say to Frances.

"I can't tell her. She'll blow it way out of proportion just like she always does." She thought.

"Liar! I didn't see you! You never intended to come. You just wanted to shut me up!"

Rachel shook her head sideways, but of course, Frances could not see her. Frances sighed deeply then continued to vent her frustration upon Rachel.

"I told them you were coming and you didn't even show to say hi or introduce yourself! I spent so much time bragging and boasting about how great you were, only to put my foot in my mouth because you didn't care enough to show!"

Frances was clearly upset with Rachel who thought it was a good thing she couldn't see her face or she would have confessed to her about Sean. Frances' voice was full of disappointment and trembled as if she was fighting off tears but she continued to reveal her feelings to Rachel, who in turn remained silent.

"Well, don't worry. I won't ask you to do anything else to help me celebrate anything ever again!"

Frances said barely able to speak from the emotions she was feeling then suddenly she became angry. She accused Rachel of being less than what she should be. She wanted to hurt and embarrass Rachel just the same as she felt last night. Rachel too fought with her emotions but allowed Frances to vent further without interruption.

"Some Christian you are! You're just a fraud and a terrible liar just like everyone else on this planet! Of course, I had to find this out the hard way and THAT hurts the most. You let me down, Rae. I never thought...YOU would let me down."

Frances hung up the phone angrily, leaving Rachel standing there against the cold wall of her apartment in silence. She had almost told Frances that she was there. She thought that she should, but if she HAD told her, Frances would know about Sean.

Rachel didn't want Frances to know about Sean because Frances enjoyed teasing her most of the time, so telling her about Sean was just asking for more torture. Rachel was not fond of that idea at all, but still she didn't want Frances to be angry with her.

She remembered an incident from high school where she told Frances about a boy that she liked.

The boy whose name was Sebastian was in her history class. He sat next to her on their first day of school and within a few weeks, he asked her out. Rachel was surprised that he did. She didn't think her parents would allow her to date since Frances drove them crazy with the whole thing. Rachel didn't bother to ask them, but she did tell Frances that she wished she could date him. Frances was less receptive than she thought her parents would be.

"Why do you like him? He's ugly! He has a huge nose, wears glasses, his ears stick out like Dumbo the elephant, and I don't think he even heard of the word ... 'shower'! Rae, you could do so much better than that guy!" Frances said as if she were trying to contain her overall disgust with Sebastian.

Rachel thought the boy was nice and his appearance wasn't as bad as Frances had made it sound, plus he was very polite and didn't say bad things about her unlike Frances' boyfriends. She also didn't think he smelled bad at all. He smelled clean while guys that Frances thought were interesting smelled like they drowned themselves in aftershave. Rachel knew Frances said those things to make her lose interest in the boy, but she didn't know why.

Rachel could have pointed all that out to her but there was just no such thing as winning an argument with Frances, especially when she was younger. Rachel began to avoid Sebastian, changed her seat in class and ignored him even though he had asked her out. She decided to do this because she didn't want Frances to tease either of them about his asking her out. He naturally began to wonder why she was obviously avoiding him and wanted to find out why.

When he asked her how she was doing after class one day, she ran off without responding to him. He didn't approach her after that, but he did smile at her occasionally which made Rachel feel terrible, so she eventually explained that her parents were very strict and did not allow her to date. He was relieved to find out that it wasn't his fault and didn't ask her out again but he let her know that he wanted to be friends. He also let her know that he thought she was the prettiest girl in the school. The next year, they did not have classes together, but he waved at her every time he saw her when they changed classes.

Rachel had never teased Frances about any of her boyfriends simply because she knew Frances would win the argument. When Rachel spotted Frances with boys, she just shook her head and continued walking by until Frances called her over to introduce them.

When one of Frances' boyfriends thought it was a good idea to hug her, Frances jumped up and slapped him hard. The boy stepped back and looked at her as if she were crazy, but so did Rachel. Frances was furious. She clenched her fists as if preparing for a fight as she spoke angrily to the young man.

"That's my little sister! Don't you put your nasty ass hands on her!" She snapped at him.

The boy stared at her, but didn't argue with Frances at all. He was rendered unable to speak from the shock of her attack upon him.

Rachel was just as amazed as the boy was when Frances quickly took hold of Rachel's arm and walked home with her leaving the boy standing there with the look of astonishment upon his face. Rachel didn't understand why Frances did that and Frances never revealed to her anything other than she is simply supposed to keep her safe from men which she had managed to do successfully until they went to college.

There, Rachel managed to sneak a relationship in while Frances was busy partying.

The relationship was not a good one for Rachel or the guy in question and like many college relationships ended with a bang. Justin didn't treat her badly, but she just didn't feel as drawn to him as other girls obviously were. He felt like it was a struggle to get her to talk to him even though she just agreed to everything he said. He felt like he was dating a zombie when he was with Rachel.

When Rachel met Justin, she wasn't too impressed with him. She knew he was a ladies' man, or that is what other people said about him, when he approached her.

Her curiosity led her to go out with him and of course, followed up with what was her inevitable first sexual experience. Rachel was not impressed with that either, but her curiosity was at least satisfied. Immediately after they had sex, she told him she didn't want to see him anymore and he was fine with that.

Then, of course, Frances found out and Justin got into loads of trouble about it. She trashed his car by scraping keys all across it, poking holes in his tires, throwing rocks at his windows then even borrowed a baseball bat to beat the car herself. She constantly spread nasty rumors about him over the following days and told everyone that he raped her sister. Then when she spotted him walking, she attacked him physically. This incident ended badly for Justin because when a few of Frances' male friends saw her attack him, they rushed to her rescue believing he was causing trouble for her. The commotion led a bystander to call the police.

 Justin was cuffed immediately when the police arrived at the scene.

"Hey! I'm the victim here! She attacked me, then they jumped in it! I didn't even touch her!" Justin said as the police cuffed him and escorted him to the squad car.

"He raped my sister! That bastard! I want to press charges against him!" Frances shouted angrily as the officer held her back keeping her from further harming Justin.

"What about my car? She totally trashed it!"

"That is her car isn't it? The caller said the car was hers." asked one of the officers.

"What? No! That's my car! She damaged it like that! I have the registration and the keys! It's mine! I can prove it! Just...wait a minute."

Justin shook his head. He could not believe that Frances had done all this to make him look bad. He was about to be arrested for rape and destruction of property, but Rachel rushed to the scene and intervened on his behalf. She told everyone that it wasn't rape in spite of her sister's rage.

When the police threatened to arrest Frances after they released Justin, Rachel told them that she did not know the whole story but simply reacted to what she believed to be true, so the police dismissed the incident with warnings for everyone since none of them were arrested before.

They told Frances she had to pay for the damages she did to his car within two weeks or they would come back and take her to jail. They told everyone else to go about their business. Justin didn't even file assault charges against anyone when they asked if he wanted to. He was just glad to be done with the whole misunderstanding. He gathered his scattered papers and books as quickly as he could and silently left the area.

Frances was angry with Rachel for telling the truth, but Rachel helped her pay for the damages she did to Justin's car, so she quickly forgave her.

Justin slowly regained his status among his peers and totally ignored both Frances and Rachel for the rest of that year then left the college. He later sent Rachel a thank you note for telling everyone the truth instead of going along with her "crazy sister". He told her in the letter to her that he was thankful that she stood up for him and that he was sorry things ended so badly for them. He also invited her to keep in touch with him, but she threw the letter away, along with his contact information.

Rachel felt sorry for him at first, but thought he wasn't worth stressing over so she quickly returned to her law studies.

Now, Rachel was feeling that strange sexual stimulation again. It wasn't necessarily curiosity, but it was definitely on a sexual level. Sean had awakened this sensation inside of her and she was fighting hard against yielding to it.

Rachel had only wanted to put the ordeal with Sean behind her but now she was facing losing the companionship of her sister in order to keep the whole incident a secret.

"Oh why did I even go? Why? Everything is … What's the use? I'll always be alone…… Always!"

Rachel could not stand the thought of being alone. She felt as if everyone on the planet had turned against her now. Rachel closed her eyes in an attempt to hold back the tears that rapidly filled them as she stood there and slowly replaced the receiver to the base of the phone. She covered her face and sobbed.

Once she had cried for as long as she could, she gradually composed herself and made her way to her bedroom where she slipped into clothing that was more comfortable. She decided to have a light supper before taking a shower and going to bed. She wanted to go into the office early in the morning and focus on her work.

Rachel was a legal office assistant and employed for a very busy law office, Waters, Anthony and Mitchell. The money she made there was sufficient for her to keep her apartment, car and dress nicely. She was not quite rich, but definitely financially comfortable.

The firm she worked for, Waters, Anthony and Mitchell, Inc., hired college graduates who studied law and passed the bar exam to be assistants for their attorneys, so that they would get the experience they needed before being hired as attorneys within the firm. Rachel had been with the firm for almost 2 years now. She was looking forward to the day when her assigned attorney would okay her and she would be employed as an attorney within the firm.

"Work will definitely take my mind off of things. Just gotta get to sleep now." She said to herself softly as she settled into bed.

Work

RACHEL awakened the next morning after her "fight" with Frances to the sound of her alarm clock. She stretched and blinked slowly as she looked around her bedroom. There was a long day ahead of her, so she needed to prepare for it. She reluctantly slid out of her bed and began to straighten it immediately, then she took a nice hot shower.

Rachel lived alone ever since her parents had died and hated it immensely. Living alone made her feel as if she were unloved by everyone and unimportant to society, in other words she was a waste of a life. She didn't like feeling that way because it was so depressing. She became a Christian to help her deal with those emotions so she could handle living alone now, but she still missed her parents greatly.

Frances had left the family home before the deaths of their parents. After having a bitter argument with their father, Frances moved into the college campus and then once they died, Rachel did the same. Rachel had stayed the night there with Frances a few times, but once her parents had died, she didn't want to be in the family home alone. She and Frances shared a dorm room for a while, but Frances was much too wild for Rachel to live with every day, so she moved into her own room after a few months.

Rachel didn't know all the details of the argument between Frances and her father, but knowing how Frances was, she was quite sure it was related to curfew being broken.

Rachel thought about her parents, as she got ready for work.

Her father, Victor Jensen, was a pleasant man most of the time. When he was angered, he was like another person though. Rachel had the sense enough not to make him direct his anger toward her, but Frances was constantly trying his patience.

Victor loved his daughters immensely. He often brought home gifts and candy for them when they were younger and scolded them when they did not do chores or get good grades in school. He adjusted his schedule as a self-employed carpenter to attend all of their important school events. He was proud of both his daughters and worked hard to provide everything they needed. He eventually became the owner of his own carpentry business and was able to hire a few employees to work with him, but when he became too old to do the work, he sold it and retired.

Rachel's mother, Paula, was also proud of her daughters. She taught them how to behave like ladies and took them to church every Sunday in spite of Frances' constant protesting. She made sure they got to school and had everything that they needed to have for assignments and projects. She was a quiet lady sometimes, but some of the things she said made her roar like a lion. She didn't have to yell or display anger to get her point across because the words she spoke were very strong.

Victor and Paula did not argue in front of their children. They displayed only love and affection. Rachel never heard them arguing even when she was a teenager. They usually agreed on everything, but when they didn't feel the same, they simply talked it over until an agreement was reached and they did this without yelling at each other. Rachel wanted that kind of relationship for herself. However lately she began to lose hope of ever having one.

While Rachel was in college, Victor died of cardiac failure then a few months after he died, Paula suffered from a stroke, then a week later fell into a coma and never recovered from it. She was officially pronounced dead after a week of life support.

Rachel hated that her parents were gone. She had enjoyed talking to them, but now she felt like she had no one again. She had gotten her mother a cat, which she affectionately named "Vittles". She chose a cat for her mother because cats are mostly independent animals. When her mother died, Rachel kept Vittles for herself.

Frances didn't even bother to attend the funerals for their parents. When Rachel caught up to her following their father's funeral, Frances was drunk and sharing a bed with some guy she didn't care about.

"Is this what you chose to do instead of come to the funeral Frances? This is how you honor the memory of our father?" Rachel was angered and could not hold it in.

"I don't want to honor his memory, Rae. I'm glad he's dead!" Frances slurred through her drunken stupor. Rachel was shocked to hear those words, but decided not to make a scene in front of the young man, so she left. When her mother died, she didn't expect Frances to show and was not disappointed when she didn't.

She looked around and wondered where Vittles was.

"I wonder where that crazy cat is. She's probably hiding somewhere new. It's okay, I'll find her later." Rachel rushed to her car now and began the long commute to the office.

Their family home was sold shortly after her parent's deaths because she couldn't stand all the painful memories. She loved her parents dearly so losing them both was hard for her. Her father had told her that if anything should happen to him, that Rachel would inherit the house. Upon his death, the attorney confirmed this, so Rachel, filled with grief, decided to sell the home in which she had grown up following her mother's death.

Rachel parked her car and made her way to the office. Mondays were usually busy. Everyone was running around like chickens searching through files, answering telephones, and rushing files over to the courthouse.

Rachel finally reached her desk and concentrated on her work. Her assigned attorney, Ms. Faye Burton, was not due in court until later that day. She began to put the necessary files together and was immediately lost in her work. She didn't feel alone anymore.

"Rachel, it's time. Let's go to the courthouse."

Attorney Burton said as she rushed toward the office exit. Rachel grabbed the stack of files quickly following her as she exited the building. Rachel had studied the files last week, so she knew just as much about the cases as Attorney Burton did. She always made it a point of studying the cases because she knew that if something went wrong, she would get the blame for it. She had seen it happen several times before. The Attorney gets the glory, but the assistant receives the blame.

The Pastor's Wife

CHERYL Montgomery was a very beautiful medium skin toned African American woman. She was not as thin and shapeless as Rachel, but more voluptuous and tempting to any man who spotted her. She tried to avoid men's hungry glances by concealing her sensuous curves with large unattractive clothing. However when she attended social gatherings, she was always the talk of the room. She pinned her hair up when she went to church and usually wore a hat to cover it. When at formal gatherings, she let it hang down which made her even more tempting to men. Cheryl wasn't a flirt at all, but she definitely had the beauty of one.

She waited patiently for her husband to speak with the few remaining members of the congregation, smiling politely as he spoke to them, answered questions and offered advice. He always took his time when speaking to them. She had learned through their years of marriage that she should be patient, so today was no different.

"They are our extended family and need direction. I will never turn my back on God's children." He told her once when she was ready to leave, but he hadn't spoken with everyone.

Cheryl didn't mind waiting for her husband. She had gotten used to it after five years of marriage to him. They had their share of difficulties, just as other people. Neither of them were bothered over talking to other couples who had asked for help with marital issues.

Cheryl continued to smile and shake hands as her husband's group began to dissipate. She nodded as she smiled.

"Lord willing, I'll see you next week. God Bless you." She said to the members while they walked away from the preacher and headed toward the door of the church.

The church's congregation had definitely grown over the past few years. The church began as a small one, holding up to thirty people comfortably, but actually housing only fifteen regularly. Now, that the church had been remodeled, Cheryl was amazed at how much both the congregation and the once tiny space had grown so drastically.

Cheryl's husband, Reverend Andrew Lee Montgomery was always a special man in her life. They met in high school and kept in touch throughout college. Andrew originally wanted to be a physical education instructor, exercised often which kept his body in shape and had not changed physically since the day they married.

Andrew's parents sometimes visited the church to support their son. Andrew's light skin color was attributed to his mother, Debra, who is Caucasian but his father, Edward, is African American. They are almost inseparable and Andrew had wanted that kind of relationship for himself so he married Cheryl.

Andrew spent most of his time away from church in preparation of future sermons reading and studying the Bible tirelessly. Andrew enjoyed studying the Bible as much as he enjoyed sharing his knowledge with others who had questions.

Cheryl was just as proud of him as he was of her. His employment as an Engineer kept them living comfortably, but she wanted to work simply because she was bored sometimes.

The congregation holds them in such high regard that Cheryl often feels pressured. She wanted to uphold the image of a good wife, but she wondered if she could. She also knew that the others did not intentionally cause her to feel this way, but she felt the fear of being categorized just the same. She was always polite and smiled at gatherings both away from and at church. She wanted to be perfect in everyone's eyes.

As she and her husband made the long journey to their home, she stared out the window of the passenger's seat. She didn't feel like talking to Andrew and he was tired as well, so they rode along in silence during most of the trip. He placed one hand on top of hers as it rested upon the armrest between them. She started then turned slowly looking into his face as he smiled.

"Cheryl, you are truly a blessing from The Lord. I don't know what I would do without you."

Cheryl looked at him and tried hard to smile but failed. The look she gave him was more of a puzzled stare than a happy one. He smiled proudly at her as she turned her head away from him and continued to stare out of the window, but said nothing in response to him. Now it was his turn to wear the puzzled stare.

"Cheryl..." he began, but she cut him off.

"I'm fine. I just need to rest."

When they arrived at their home, she rushed out of the car before he could open the door for her. She wanted to run as far away from him as she could, but her body was too tired to move that way. She climbed the stairs, opened the door quickly disappearing inside the immaculate house as he closed the passenger door of the car, watching her distance herself from him in silence.

Cheryl rushed to her bedroom and began to remove her clothes. She tossed them on the bed and slipped into the shower. She needed to relax, to think and to forget at the same time. She began to remember her past mistakes, flaws and imperfections. She wasn't as secure as everyone else had thought her to be. She had never told anyone her secret, not even God. She knew he didn't need to be told, but she never confessed it before him. Tears began to trickle from her eyes as she held her head beneath the running water from the shower. Her life was becoming more and more complicated and she was helpless to prevent the imminent disaster that she felt was drawing closer.

Andrew walked into the house and looked around. Cheryl had made her way directly up the stairs. She hadn't even bothered to check the messages. He looked at the stairs, still confused by what happened in the car.

"Cheryl Lynnette...what is going on with you?" he thought as he turned his attention to the telephone and began to listen to the messages.

Cheryl got out of the shower and slipped into a clean robe. She was sitting in front of the vanity when Andrew walked into the room and began to remove his suit jacket. He looked at her reflection as she brushed her hair in front of the vanity.

"Cheryl, who is Matthew? He called and left a message on voicemail, but he didn't say what it was about."

Cheryl tried hard to conceal her terror.

"Matthew? I don't remember a Matthew. What did he say?" She slowly began to grow calm again.

"He didn't say a lot. He said Hello Cheryl this is Matthew and I have something for you. He didn't say anything else. He called from a private number and he didn't leave a callback number either."

Andrew was not angry or suspicious, but simply curious about whom Matthew was. Cheryl turned and looked at him slowly.

"Matthew must be the homeless man I saw when I was shopping the other day. I gave him the number and told him to call us so that he could talk to you. He didn't leave a number because he doesn't have one and most payphones show as private on the caller ID."

Andrew nodded in silence and didn't think anything more about it. Cheryl on the other hand was a mental wreck. She had lied to her husband and she was feeling badly about it.

"Oh, okay. Well, I will definitely try to find him and talk to him. Maybe he needs a ride to the church. We could pick him up next Sunday, if we can get a hold of him. You did a very good job, Honey. Everyone needs to know about God's love. Homeless people too. Maybe we can help him find an affordable place to live or give him a job cleaning the church for us. He could stay there until he saves enough to get another place. What do you think of that?"

Andrew had shared so many ideas with Cheryl, he knew she would be happy with at least one of them, but Cheryl barely acknowledged him. She smiled as if she were in a daze and nodded as he stared at her and waited for her opinion, which she never revealed.

She slowly rose from her seat in front of the vanity as Andrew continued to get undressed. She walked slowly toward the bedroom door. She did not stop until he called out to her.

"Cheryl is everything okay? I mean, you seem very distant."

"I was just thinking about Rachel. She is having trouble, but she doesn't want to talk about it. I don't know how I can get through to her. I know things have been hard for her since her mother died, but she doesn't even talk to anyone in church. She sat there today and stared at everyone as if ... well, she was someplace where she did not belong."

"Really? She left service before I could get a chance to talk to her. I will make sure to check on her. Maybe I should stop by and see her tomorrow."

Andrew was always concerned about his congregation and often made special house calls to those he and Cheryl felt were in need of assistance. He did not mind giving his followers financial assistance, or any other kind of help. He was a very generous and caring man.

"I think calling her first is a good idea, but perhaps I should visit with her instead. I will give her a call and tell her that I will stop by tomorrow." Cheryl volunteered as Andrew nodded in agreement.

"Okay, that sounds like a good idea. Rachel may feel more comfortable talking to you."

"I think she is going to be uncomfortable, but I may be able to get her to relax enough to talk to me."

Cheryl walked out of the bedroom and headed down the stairs to the kitchen as Andrew changed his clothes, headed to the basement then began his exercise routine. The stairs that led to the basement were also in the living room area, so he didn't have to come through the kitchen to reach the basement.

Cheryl knew he wouldn't talk to her long because he had done the same thing for five years. He wasn't very spontaneous at all. He preferred having plans made ahead of time.

Whenever they took vacations, he had to write out schedules of what they would do and followed the written plans to the letter. He couldn't tolerate things being in disarray.

Cheryl went to the living room, listened as Andrew began to lift his weights and picked up the telephone. She whispered into the receiver.

"Hello, it's me. I told you not to call me here! What has gotten into you?" she watched the stairs as she spoke into the telephone.

"Never mind all that. I will stop by and see you tomorrow. I have errands to run, so I should get there around 2 PM. That is all I can spare and don't call here again!" she hung up the phone and sighed loudly as she closed her eyes.

Cheryl heard Andrew walking up the stairs once his workout was done and quickly headed back to the kitchen. She listened as he turned on the shower then she poured herself a glass of wine and drank it down fast before pouring herself another. She leaned against the counter for support, closed her eyes and breathed hard in an attempt to compose herself.

After a few minutes, Andrew came down the stairs wearing his robe. Cheryl stood in the kitchen sipping her glass of wine. She looked at him as he looked around for her then spotted her. She smiled weakly.

"All done for the day?" she asked before taking another sip.

"Yeah, I think I need to start another routine. This one isn't wearing me out like it did when I first started it." He said.

Cheryl nodded then placed her glass on the counter.

"Well, I suppose an upgrade is in order then, Dear." She said as she walked out of the kitchen. Andrew watched her curiously as she walked by him.

"Cheryl, I feel like I am chasing you around the house. Is there something else on your mind?"

"I just wanted a sip of wine. Why would you think something is wrong? You aren't chasing me around the house. You live here too. Relax Andrew. Sometimes thoughts that I have are not about you. It's not anything to worry yourself over."

Cheryl walked up the stairs, quickly slipped into her nightgown then into bed. She didn't want to be awake when Andrew came to bed.

Andrew knew Cheryl was trying to escape him and decided not to pursue her. He went into his home office next to the kitchen and began to work on his next sermon. By the time he was done, Cheryl was fast asleep. He slipped into his pajamas and lay in bed next to her. He looked over at her for a moment, then turned away slowly and drifted off to sleep.

Temptation

THE NEXT morning, Andrew arose early. He had to get to work quickly and wanted to avoid the heavier traffic. He walked briskly to the bathroom and prepared for the long day ahead.

Cheryl stretched slowly and sat upright in bed. She blinked her eyes adjusting them to the sunlight that now filled the bedroom and reached for her robe. She placed her feet into her slippers then slowly rose to her feet as Andrew rushed out of the bathroom making his way directly to the closet.

Andrew glanced over at her, as he quickly got dressed.

"Good morning, Sweetheart. You don't have to get out of bed, I can get breakfast myself. Thanks anyway. You just relax today. I think you need to take a break. You're too distracted, especially lately." Andrew said as he slipped into his jeans and tee shirt.

Cheryl barely looked at him. She rubbed her eyes attempting to avoid contact with him.

"I'm fine, Andrew. I'm just off to a slow start. I'm fine. I think you worry too much about me. I wish you wouldn't do that."

Andrew looked at her strangely, then spoke.

"Yes, I worry about you, but I do that because you are my wife. Should a husband not worry about his wife if she is acting strangely? I'm concerned about your well-being just as I should be until you convince me to do otherwise." Andrew didn't raise his voice, but he did show his concern while he spoke to her.

Cheryl was beginning to grow agitated.

"There is no need to worry. I have already told you that I am fine. Everything is fine. Please stop stressing over unnecessary things. You won't be able to concentrate on work."

Andrew shook his head slightly as he sighed deeply in defeat.

"Okay, I can't talk about it anyway now or I'll be late. I will have to talk to you later."

Andrew walked to her and took her into his arms. He leaned forward to kiss her but she instinctively turned away causing his kiss to land on her cheek. He released her immediately and looked at her.

"Why did you do that?" he questioned. "She never stopped me from kissing her before." Andrew thought as he waited for her reply. Cheryl immediately smiled as if she were being a tease.

"If you start something now, you can't finish it, so get to work you." Cheryl said playfully. Andrew smiled back. He liked the way she teased him.

"Right. I'll call you during my lunch hour, if I'm not busy working through it." He said as he kissed her cheek once more then walked out the bedroom door smiling back at her.

"I love you, Cheryl." Andrew said.

"Get going you tease!" Cheryl scrunched her nose playfully then walked to the door of the bedroom, waving at him as he left the house.

Cheryl sighed deeply. She was glad to be alone now as she sat on the bed and listened for Andrew's truck to leave. When she couldn't hear it anymore, she took a quick shower, got dressed and headed to her own car.

Cheryl began her day by visiting a home for senior citizens. She had a group of people that she would speak with on a weekly basis. They were all women and very sweet to her. She sometimes bought them pictures from the vacations she and her husband had experienced before. They really enjoyed seeing the pictures of the couple together.

After talking to the women for a while, she stopped by a fancy Italian cuisine restaurant and had lunch alone. She wanted to think, but all her thoughts only led her to more questions, so she began to try not to think.

A dark haired Italian waiter served her as she looked around at the other people in the restaurant. He smiled at her gently touching her hand as she frowned at him. He smirked slightly then walked away.

Cheryl looked around at the other customers again and began to remember how happy she was when she and Andrew first got married. She knew she could not live without him, but she didn't enjoy her life with him either. She thought she needed something more, or was she just being selfish.

After leaving the restaurant, she drove to a nearby hotel and checked into a room. She made her way to the room and sat down on the sofa inside the living section. She poured herself a glass of wine and took a sip. A few minutes later, there was a knock on the door. She rose to her feet gradually making her way to the door and opening it. There stood the waiter from the restaurant who had touched her hand.

"I thought I told you before not to call my house. Matthew, why would you do such a stupid and foolhardy thing! You know....." She said angrily but he cut her off.

"Yeah, but you weren't returning my calls to your cell. I had to reach you." He replied smiling at her.

She frowned angrily as he moved closer toward her, but still unable to enter the sanctuary offered inside the room. She held the door tightly in place, as he looked at her then the door. She breathed deep breaths as if she were trying to calm herself. He placed one palm against the door, gazing at her as seductively as possible.

"Aren't you going to let me in?" he whispered.

Cheryl frowned, but then huffed, crossed her arms in front of her chest and turned away from the door as he gently pushed it wide enough for his entry. Once inside, he slowly shut the door behind him never taking his eyes off her even though her back was to him.

"Okay, I won't do that again. I just wanted to see you. Am I forgiven now?" Matthew spoke softly as he approached her. She turned and faced him slowly.

"You really don't know what you have done, do you? Everything could have been ruined because of your brainless action. How could you have been so stupid! You can't threaten me like this forever, Matthew. I will not allow it."

"I didn't mean it as a threat. I just wanted to see you, that's all. Don't be angry. You said yourself that I am young and impulsive, but you also said that was one of my charms. C'mon, I'll help you relax a bit."

He immediately began to massage her shoulders. Cheryl had definitely been tense and a massage would have been nice, but she knew better than to trust Matthew with the task. However, she couldn't tell him "No." She hadn't been able to before, so she knew she wouldn't do it today either.

More Sin

A FEW HOURS later, Cheryl was home again making dinner for Andrew. She couldn't concentrate on her cooking and did not notice that the chicken baking in the oven began to burn. She stood in front of the stove stirring the pasta boiling in water, but thinking about what happened earlier that day.

Cheryl could still feel his hands sliding along her arms gently caressing her as he attempted to soothe her fit of anger. She felt as if his body was pressed closely to hers as he whispered into her ear.

"Shhhhh, now. It's okay. I'll take care of you."

His lips gently grazed her neck sending tremors down her spine. She felt her body responding to his touch in spite of her mind's protests. His hands caressed her gently, slowly undoing her blouse. She was lost in his touch and surrendered in his hold. She was so deep in thought that when Andrew walked in and called out to her, she didn't respond.

"Cheryl...I'm..." he began, but stopped in his tracks when he smelled the burning chicken.

He rushed to the kitchen expecting to find her hurt or unconscious, but she stood there humming softly to herself.

Andrew's face was full of worry. He shook his head slightly, looking at her again. She was clearly unaware of what was going on around her. The pasta that she stirred began to boil over, yet she stood there unmoving. Andrew had to get to her or she would be injured.

"Cheryl?"

Andrew walked over to her quickly, gently touching her shoulder. She started, gasped loudly and dropped the stirring spoon.

"Oh! Andrew, I didn't hear you come in. How was your day?" She asked as she squatted to pick up the spoon.

Andrew watched her in silence as she slowly rose, straightening her body then walked over to the sink. She dropped the spoon inside and began to search for another one. She was still thinking about the afternoon, but didn't want Andrew to see her face. She knew she would feel guilty about it if she looked at him. She turned on the water and washed her hands in an effort to keep her back to him.

Andrew continued to watch her in silence as she kept her back to him. Then he grabbed a towel and removed the burnt chicken from the oven. He knew something was bothering her, but he also had a feeling that she would not talk to him about it. Andrew decided that whatever was bothering her, he needed to let her work it out until she was ready to tell him about it.

Andrew didn't want to argue with Cheryl because he hated doing that. Somehow he knew that her behavior had stemmed from the argument they had a few weeks before. His head dropped in shame as he felt his heart begin to ache. He wanted her to love him, as he loved her, but he knew that she was much too angry, hurt and disappointed in him now. He knew she would not allow him to touch her and she would offer him no comfort. He sighed deeply as he fought for the right words to say. He didn't want to lose her, but he wanted her to not feel pressured by him.

"Cheryl, I know you want to keep whatever is bothering you to yourself, so I won't question you again. I just want you to know that whenever you are ready to talk to me about it, I will listen because I love you. For now, I'm going to give you the space and time you need."

 Andrew placed the towel on the table and walked out of the kitchen silently. He barely even breathed as he made his way up the stairs clearly in a saddened state. He changed into his sweat pants for his workout then headed to the basement.

Cheryl watched him walking up the stairs and knew he was about to start his work out session which he always did when he was frustrated or according to his schedule.

Andrew knew Cheryl was not happy with their marriage. He could tell from her behavior. He wanted to make Cheryl happy, but he felt as if he had failed. He remembered the last argument they had during his workout.

"Why? Why can't we be like normal couples sexually? What is wrong with it? We are only human. Why can't WE enjoy sex? Sex is not a sin, you know."

"We can enjoy sex, Cheryl, but that is not the way. I do not believe THAT is necessary or right. Why don't you enjoy normal sex? Is it me? I don't please you? You can tell me."

"I've already told you and once again, you aren't listening. I'm done talking to you Andrew. I am a woman with needs. I need more than what I'm getting from you, but you expect me to be happy about it? You don't seem to mind so much when I'm pleasuring you, but you can't....."

"Stop that, Cheryl! I told you before that you don't have to do that! Now you want to blame me because you insist upon doing it? That is not fair, Cheryl! I never asked you to…"

"That's my point exactly, Andrew! You shouldn't have to ask for it and neither should I. For goodness sake, WE ARE MARRIED! I don't think it's wrong if it makes you happy. You should feel the same way about me, but obviously, you don't think I'm worth it…or this marriage. You think God will look at you and say you are dirty or sinful because you did…."

"This is ridiculous Cheryl. I'm not going to use my mouth like THAT. This is just too much. I don't want to argue anymore."

"Ah! There we have it! Andrew who won't please his wife. So I have to let it go because you say so. I've listened to you for five grueling years, constantly telling me why you can't do things to please me. I know it's just because you don't think I'm worth it. God won't condemn you for pleasing me, but you will condemn yourself instead! You don't think I'm worth it! I don't deserve to be happy… Just be honest about it Andrew!"

Andrew sighed loudly, threw up his hands in frustration and began his exercise routine at that point. Cheryl stormed out of the exercise room, slamming the door loudly behind her. Andrew stopped his routine and looked at the door. He knew she was angry with him for not being like the men she had dated before. He wanted to please her sexually, but he truly believed as stated in

Ephesians 5:3 that fellatio and cunnilingus were simply sinful.

After he finished his workout, he made his way upstairs, took a shower and got ready for bed. He didn't want to upset Cheryl any more than she already was with him. He wanted to wait for her to patiently come to him and talk in spite of the fact that lately she had been easily upset by the slightest thing he did.

"I told her that I would give her some space so maybe I should not sleep here."

He began to wonder why Cheryl was acting so strangely to him other than the argument. She had gotten to the point where she could not stand the sight of him. She barely looked at him during church yesterday and then again this evening after work. She behaved as if she found him to be repulsive. In the car on the way home, she all but screamed when he touched her hand.

"Did she have another reason to feel anger toward him?" he thought as he made his way to the guest bedroom.

Andrew began to think about what he could have possibly done to hurt her and make her so cold to him. She behaved as if she didn't love him anymore and couldn't stand the sight of him. He began to believe that her distance toward him had something to do with this person, "Matthew", but he did not want to believe that his wife would do anything to hurt him like that.

Yet somehow, deep down inside, he could feel that was the case.

Cheryl was miserable with their sex life, as she had told him repeatedly and sought pleasure from someone who was willing to give her what she wanted, what she deserved.

Andrew breathed hard as he thought. He wasn't happy with the thoughts, but they made sense to him now. He began to blame himself for making her miserable enough to betray him.

Andrew was broken hearted, but could not confront his wife. He told himself that he should wait until she was ready to talk to him about it. He told himself to not interfere even at the risk of losing her permanently. He had to be patient and allow her to decide if she wanted to continue to keep this affair a secret or if she wanted to tell him and try to save their marriage.

 He finally dozed off to sleep in the guest room for the night.

When Cheryl finished cleaning the kitchen, she was exhausted. She walked into the dark bedroom expecting Andrew to be waiting for her. She didn't turn on the light because she didn't want to disturb his sleep, or talk to him. She simply wanted to sleep now.

She quickly took a shower, changed into her gown and headed for bed. She eased into the king sized bed, attempting not to awaken Andrew, who was being very quiet for some reason. She felt as if the bed was unusually cold tonight. She slowly reached over to his side of the bed with her finger tips and felt nothing.

"Andrew?" she whispered.

She heard no response so she called out again.

"Andrew? Are you here?"

There was still no reply. She sat up in the bed and turned on the light. Andrew was not there.

Cheryl's eyes grew wide in surprise. They had slept in the same bed for five years even when they argued, but tonight, they both slept alone. Cheryl looked around the room, which seemed to grow larger, just as her misery did. She hadn't meant to hurt her husband, but that was unavoidable now. She knew Andrew was not stupid, but that is exactly what she had hoped for. She knew she could not go on pretending that things were great between them.

Cheryl closed her eyes slowly as her loneliness engulfed her. She knew she had pushed Andrew away through her constant rejection of him over the past few weeks, but she didn't know why she felt bad about it. After all, he had rejected her before so it was only natural for her to do the same, wasn't it? She slowly slid beneath the covers, turned out the light while crying silently until she began to drift off into sleep.

"I'm so sorry Andrew. I'm sorry for everything." She thought as she closed her eyes and fell asleep.

It was late the next morning when Cheryl awakened. She hadn't set her alarm to go off, but she didn't mind the sleep. She got out of bed and began to make her way to the kitchen. Andrew was not there now, but he had definitely been there. He left coffee in the pot, but it was cold now. Cheryl began to feel bad again. Andrew had always kissed her goodbye before going to work, he didn't do it today though.

Cheryl sat in a chair and stared in the distance. She felt as if her life were falling apart before her eyes. There had to be a way to stop this insanity. She couldn't think clearly at all. Suddenly she heard a buzzing sound and quickly turned to find the source. She looked down at her cell phone on the counter and gasped.

"Oh no! If Andrew saw this…"

She didn't dare to finish that statement. She quickly snatched the phone up from the counter.

"Matthew! Just stop it!"

She threw the phone against the wall angrily then collapsed to her knees. She couldn't control herself now.

She sobbed loudly, covering her face as her guilt and shame consumed her.

"Please! Leave me alone! Just make it stop!" she sobbed loudly.

Things Change

A FEW days later, Rachel was on her way to the courthouse again. Rachel looked at Faye who only carried an empty briefcase. Rachel knew the briefcase was empty because she carried all the files in her own briefcase. Faye wanted to look important.

Rachel scoffed as she waited while Faye stopped to speak to another attorney from a different firm. The first of Faye's cases was about to start and she was going to be late unless Rachel could interrupt her.

"Attorney Burton, we are up very soon. We must be on our way now." Rachel said as politely as she could. Faye looked at the clock on the wall.

"She's right. I'll have to talk to you after I win this case. Good luck to you Bernard." Faye said politely smiling as she shook the attorney's hand. He smiled back and shook her hand.

"Same to you, but I don't think you'll need it." He said in reply. Faye immediately turned toward Rachel and walked past her into the courtroom.

Faye was a blond woman with green eyes and very slender so she always got lots of attention. Rachel thought that the reason why Faye had won so many cases was because she distracted everyone so well with her appearance.

Whenever they entered the courtroom, Faye strutted like a peacock making sure that all the eyes in the courtroom were upon her

"That's all Rachel. Thank you. You can take your seat back there now. I'll call you if I need anything." She said softly as they set up for the first case.

Faye would never share the spotlight at all. Rachel gathered her notes as the opposing attorney walked over to them smiling politely at Rachel, then addressed Faye.

"Hello Faye. I just wanted to say good luck. You just may need it today. This judge may not be so easy to convince. I heard Judge Whittaker is going through some uh...personal issues we'll call it. So he may not be in such a good mood to see such a well decorated woman like you."

"Michael, I don't need advice from you. I would appreciate it if you would save the talk for after I've won again."

Michael smiled then winked at her. Faye blushed slightly then quickly turned away. She was trying to keep Rachel from seeing it, but it was too late.

"What?" Rachel thought. "She and him....oh no! This is not going to go well at all."

A few hours later, Rachel made her way back to the office alone. Faye did not want to walk with her now. Rachel never interfered with Faye's courtroom antics before, so today was a definite first.

The judge was not impressed with Faye's presentation. Rachel had to intervene and quickly presented information from the files and her notes that other people had overlooked. Rachel's points won the case, not Faye.

Faye was much too embarrassed to be seen with Rachel afterwards, so she stormed out of the courtroom before Rachel who was now quite sure that Faye was waiting to have her unjustly fired from the office.

When Rachel walked up to the door, she sighed deeply then pushed the doors open. All eyes were immediately upon her. She lowered her eyes to the floor as she walked toward her desk and sat down. She felt as if she were in the nightclub again and began to feel sick to her stomach.

Very soon, most of the assistants in the office were praising Rachel.

"Wait a minute everyone. I don't want anyone to misunderstand what actually happened. Faye is the attorney. I was there to help her in a moment when she was at a loss for words. I wasn't trying to embarrass her or get back at her. I was helping her to win the case, that's what we do. It wasn't a vicious plot, scheme or plan. We won the case and that is what I wanted to do for this company not to embarrass a star attorney. Besides, Faye is not like that. She will be proud of what I did and she will not ..."

Before Rachel could finish her words, Faye approached the group that had gathered around her and interrupted loudly.

"Rachel! You are wanted in the Mitchell office. Get there promptly! The rest of you, if you want to continue to work here, get back to your desks!"

Faye snapped sharply at everyone who congratulated Rachel on her win. She stood there frowning angrily as the others made their way slowly back to their desks.

Rachel rose from her desk slowly followed closely by Faye. As they neared the door to the office, Faye's anger began to rear its ugly head.

"This will teach you to stand me up in a courtroom again! In fact, you may never see the inside of another courtroom for what you've done to me today!" She said smugly.

Rachel glanced back at her in surprise. She didn't think it was that much of a deal, but apparently, it was.

"Am I really about to lose my job because of this woman's incompetence?" Rachel wondered.

Faye stared at Rachel angrily in return. She stepped closer to her frowning hard as she spoke to Rachel.

"Stupid girl, you could have had everything, now, you've blown it! You should have kept your mouth shut and let me handle the case. Your career is officially over! You will never be an attorney...not in this town. I'll see to that myself! You'll be lucky if another firm accepts you as an assistant."

Rachel could not believe what Faye was saying to her. Faye frowned at her then opened the door to the Mitchell office and pushed her way past Rachel practically knocking her down as she walked inside.

Rachel wanted to be a lawyer ever since she was a little girl and now, Faye had threatened to make sure that her dream would never come true. She walked into the office with her eyes on the floor. She didn't want to look at anyone as she fought the tears that were building up in her eyes. Faye smiled wickedly. Her face was filled with satisfaction at seeing Rachel so visibly upset.

"This is her. She's the one who made me look bad in court today. She gave me files that did not contain the right information so I studied the false information. She made me look like a total idiot today. This imbecile needs to be removed from this firm effective immediately." Faye had stated her case and all the eyes in the boardroom turned to Rachel.

"Is this true Ms. Jensen? Did you attempt to deliberately make one of our top attorneys look bad in court by giving her the wrong information?" The president of the board of directors asked as he looked directly at Rachel. She slowly lifted her head after saying a quick prayer.

"I must first apologize for the incident gentlemen. It was not my intention that this happened, not at all, but I must speak the truth here. I gave Ms. Burton…."

Faye immediately interrupted her.

"That's… 'Attorney Burton' Rachel. Remember my title when you address me!"

"I was speaking to the board members, not you therefore, I was not addressing you. Please don't interrupt me again, thank you, Ms. Burton." Rachel was clearly fed up with Faye's behavior now and she didn't care how she spoke to her.

Faye frowned at Rachel, but continued to interrupt.

"Do you see? Do you see how incompetent SHE is? THIS, is what I have had to deal with every day! She did this deliberately! She can't even address me correctly! Why have I been given such an imbecile to work with me? She was plotting to make me look bad in court when she is not worthy of standing in my shadow! Then, just now when I was going to get her for this meeting, she was gloating about it with her co-workers! They were all gathered around her desk listening to her talk about me. She has always wanted to embarrass me and now that she has done it, she is attempting, rather poorly I might add, to make it all appear to be some terrible mistake. I want her removed from this firm immediately! She is highly incompetent and shallow."

Rachel clenched her fists tightly.

"God give me strength." She thought as she shut her eyes and fought hard to keep from swinging at Faye.

"That is not true at all! That's not what was happening!"

Rachel said pleadingly.

Faye scoffed loudly.

"Yeah, right!"

The President of the board rose from his seat and walked over to Rachel. The other board members were nodding as they spoke to each other. Rachel could tell they were convinced that Faye was right. Rachel closed her eyes again and tried to calm herself.

"Continue young lady. Tell us what happened." He said as he stood in front of her.

Rachel slowly opened her eyes and looked into his. He looked familiar, but she couldn't remember why.

"I gave her a copy of the same file that I had for the case. The information I showed to the judge is exactly what she had as well. The only thing I did not give her were my personal notes on the case. I don't think Ms. Burton bothered to go over the case again though. She was probably too busy flirting with other attorneys from different law firms to study the case. I studied it Friday and found the discrepancies that I revealed to the judge, but I did not discuss them with Ms. Burton beforehand because I believed her to be intelligent enough to discover them for herself, but I was obviously wrong. What happened in the courtroom today, was a result of her lack of studying the evidence file and not my interference. I did nothing except what was expected of a good attorney in order to win a case. If I am wrong for assisting this firm with winning the case and making a client happy, then I deserve to be terminated and will accept that decision graciously. However, I do not believe that the board will fire me because I helped to earn the firm money and keep our reputation strong."

"Do you have the notes you took on this case, Rachel?" the president asked.

"They are in my file at my desk. I can get them." Rachel replied.

"I think that would be a good idea, Rachel. Go and get them while we talk to Ms. Burton."

Rachel turned and walked out of the room. Once she left the room, she began to breathe, then she noticed that the President called Faye… "Ms. Burton" just as she had. Rachel smiled. She began to feel better about the whole mess now.

When she returned, Faye was not in the office. She wanted to ask what happened, but decided against it.

The President extended his hand and accepted the files for the board to review. They looked at each other in awe, then looked at Rachel.

"Rachel, you…You didn't have any help from anyone regarding this case? These are YOUR notes, not some that you borrowed from someone else?"

"Yes, they are mine. I studied the case on Friday and that is what I discovered. Why? Is there something wrong with my notes? I simply…"

"Rachel, there is nothing wrong with these notes at all. This is quite impressive. You have done an outstanding job here. From now on, you will be taking all of Ms. Burton's files. You will be taking her place as she is resigning as of today."

Rachel could not believe her ears. She was finally going to be the full-fledged attorney she wanted to be. No longer anyone's assistant, but an attorney. She was excited beyond words.

"That is…unless you wish to remain an assistant here." The President said. Rachel immediately snapped out of it.

"No, I have wanted to be an attorney ever since I began my career here. I am very thankful. Thank you all for the chance." Rachel spoke as calmly as she could, but was very excited. The president smiled at her politely.

"We will have to hire an assistant for you though." The president began, but Rachel did not want them to do that.

"No thank you gentlemen. I prefer to do everything myself. It will give me a better feel for the cases. I do thank you for the gracious offer though. I want to thank you all again for this incredible opportunity. I will work hard and not let the firm or our clients down. Thank you very much gentlemen."

Rachel turned and walked out of the room, but before she could get to the elevator, a young woman came running up to her as quickly as she could. She leaned against the wall as Rachel watched her attempt to catch her breath. Then she spoke finally.

"Rachel, Rachel Jensen?" she said barely able to breathe from being winded.

"Yes?"

"Your new office is ready. If you will just follow me, I could show you where it is and we could begin moving your case files into it."

"New office? Oh my!" Rachel was again excited.

She followed the assistant to her new office and looked around.

She was very happy with her office and immediately reached for the telephone. She wanted to call Frances and tell her what was going on, but she stopped abruptly when she remembered that Frances was angry with her.

"I can't call her. She's not speaking to me." She sighed to herself.

The assistant waited outside of Rachel's office as the janitor placed her new black and gold nameplate on the door of her office.

"Congratulations Attorney Jensen." The janitor said after he had finished his work.

"Thank you, Jimmy. It's like a dream come true...almost." She said sadly.

"Well, don't you worry, Rae. Now that you are a uh...vital part of this fine organization, I'm sure that you will have lots of high class friends and be invited to all the parties where the rich folks get drunk and eat their fish eggs. You are very lucky."

Rachel couldn't help but snicker at Jimmy's words. She had worked for Waters, Anthony and Mitchell for nearly two years now without being invited to any of the company parties because she was just an assistant. Suddenly, her status within the company had changed and she knew Jimmy was right.

Jimmy never attended any parties, but knew about each one because he had plenty of cleaning up to do afterward. He didn't mind though. He was happy with his job and his pay. He preferred the rich attorneys to leave him alone.

Jimmy was an elderly man in his early sixties and scheduled to retire within a few months. He was looking forward to his retirement, but was glad that Rachel had accomplished her goal in life before his departure from the organization. Therefore, he felt it was appropriate to tease her, but on the inside he was quite proud. She had never been anything but kind to him ever since she had been there, so he returned the favor.

"Good luck to you Rachel and God bless. I hope this turns out to be what you really want, but in my honest opinion, you may do better for yourself if you had your own practice. You are much too smart for this place, much more deserving of something better, more human, but it's a good place for you to start your attorney career, you know. To make a name for yourself before you get your own business going."

Rachel looked at him and slightly raised an eyebrow as if she were thinking about what he had said.

"Just giving you something to think about, Rae. There's no need to rush into anything yet anyways. Take care." Jimmy said as he walked out of the office.

The assistant looked at Jimmy as he walked away, then she looked at Rachel, but did not enter into the office.

"Can I get you anything Attorney Jensen?" the assistant asked.

"Oh, I....uh...Why are you ...Wait...What is your name?" Rachel had so many questions; she didn't quite know where to begin.

The assistant looked at her strangely.

"My name is Violet. Attorney Jensen." She replied without entering the large office. Rachel rose and walked over to the door.

"Okay, Violet. Can you answer a few questions for me?"

"Yes, Attorney Jensen. I will do my best." She replied.

"Why don't you just call me Rachel? All my good friends call me Rae, so why don't you do the same. I hope that you will consider me to be a good friend too - that is if I don't drive you crazy with questions." Rachel smiled at Violet who immediately smiled back.

"Wow, I can really call you, just Rae? That has never happened before. The President of the Board told me to comply with your wishes. I am your secretary. I will be making out your schedule, you know, courtroom appointments, meetings, parties, everything, as well as typing up any memos, correspondence and anything else you may require. If you need anything, I'm the person who will get it for you."

"Wow. I never thought...Well, that's good Violet. I'm glad I have you for a secretary. I guess I better get my files and review my future cases then." Rachel said as she clapped her hands together as if shaking dust from them.

Violet smiled.

"If I may say so, Rae, you are not as uptight as those other attorneys. I have a really good feeling about you."

"Thank you Violet. I began as an assistant, but well, I'm here now. I still can't believe it myself, but...well, God is good. He did this for me and he blessed me to meet you. Now I feel like I have someone to talk to. It's really nice. I'm thankful."

"Oh, you...Well, me too. That's wonderful, Rae. I didn't think there was such a thing as an attorney who believed in God. It's quite an interesting thing. Most attorneys have to lie just to win a case, so please excuse my shock from it."

"Oh not at all. I don't mind. In fact, I would have to agree with you. Some depend on fancy talk and dazzling the judge rather than studying the case facts against the law. If they took a closer look at their cases, they would find exactly what they need to win the case."

"Really? What is that?"

"The truth. The same thing is evident in any situation. The statement, "The truth shall set you free" reminds us that there is freedom in truth. It may not be a legal thing all the time, but you will experience freedom nevertheless. Freedom from whatever is bothering us or ailing us is found in the truth. It works wonders and in several cases even miracles."

Rachel was at ease talking to Violet. Then she felt a pang in her chest.

"The truth shall set you free." She thought. "Why didn't I tell Frances the truth yesterday?"

She didn't feel so confident anymore now, but slowly made her way to her old desk followed by Violet. She and Violet moved all of her files into her new office as the other assistants who had praised her earlier stared in disbelief.

"Faye got fired and Rae took her place as an attorney! That is an amazing Cinderella story! Good for Rae! She deserved it after taking all that crap from that mindless bimbo for almost two years!"

Some of the assistants whispered amongst themselves as they applauded Rae while she moved into her new office.

Sean, Again

AFTER Rachel was done moving her files into her office, the sky began to grow dark. Violet took her seat at the secretary's desk as the phone rang and took messages while Rachel finished arranging her office. Her first few hours as an attorney and she was still arranging her office. Violet's voice interrupted her heavy disappointing sighs.

"I'm sorry to disturb you, Rae, but President Mitchell wants you to return to the board room as soon as you can. He wants you to meet the other attorneys." Violet said hurriedly.

"Oh, alright. I'm going there right now." Rachel immediately headed to the boardroom where every attorney for the organization waited anxiously to meet her.

President Mitchell approached her quickly, extending his hand to her.

"Rachel Jensen, our newest member. Welcome to the big time as they call it. I felt it was necessary for you to meet everyone because you may have to get a few tips from them or borrow a book or two occasionally."

Everyone laughed. Rachel didn't see what was funny, but smiled politely. The other attorneys all began to introduce themselves to her. Rachel felt like she was an item on display for everyone to investigate. She felt uncomfortable in spite of her smile.

"I will be glad when this is over." She thought as she smiled politely and listened to the men's meaningless chatter.

"Why don't we finish this discussion over drinks since we are done for the day? I'll buy the first round you guys. I even know a great spot where everyone can have a good time. What do you guys…," He quickly looked at Rachel then scoffed softly as he smirked then continued speaking "Oh, sorry, and little lady, say?" Russell Parks, the most prominent of all the attorneys for the firm had spoken an apology that was obviously staged.

Rachel smiled politely pretending that she didn't know he wasn't sincere.

Rachel knew Russell was the most prominent because of her studying. She made it a habit of studying the files for her assigned attorney but also studied the firm's history as well. Russell Parks had won more cases than any other attorney in the firm's history had.

Russell was a well-manicured man. He wore expensive suits, shoes and kept his hair neatly trimmed. His appearance told all about him. He was a natural winner and it was evident in everything he did. Rachel wanted to learn more from him, but had the feeling she would not be that lucky.

Naturally, the majority of the group wanted to go for drinks.

Much to Rachel's horror, they followed Russell to the same club that she had been to Saturday night. She bit her lip to hold in her gasp as her eyes widened in terror. She hoped that she would not see Sean there.

She stayed with the group who all ordered drinks, with one exception, her. She looked around in terror expecting Sean to approach her, but he didn't. Russell tapped her shoulder. She started, then turned facing him quickly.

"Hey little lady. You don't want a drink? You can have anything you want. It's my treat." He said as if he expected her to do as he asked. He smirked then lifted his drink as Rachel shook her head and declined politely. She attempted to avoid feeling like the piece of meat he obviously saw her as.

"That's very kind of you Mr. Parks, but, I'm not very thirsty. I really should get back to the office and study my case files a little more...."

"My, my, my, aren't you a worrywart? That is so old time. Don't you know people just don't operate like that anymore?" he laughed softly as Rachel stared at him as if she were trying to figure out what he was saying. Then he took a sip of his champagne smiling at her wickedly. Rachel cringed slightly, but decided to continue the conversation.

"How do you win your cases, Mr. Parks?" she asked hesitantly. She had not wanted to ask because she had feared what the answer would be, but against her better judgment, she did so anyway.

"Easily. Someday, I may tell you exactly how, that is....if you are willing to be nice about it." He said as he ran his fingertips along her upper arm.

Rachel was immediately repelled by his touch. She stepped away from him quickly trying not to cause a scene and remain calm. Her eyes grew wide in terror for a moment, but she took a deep breath and quickly composed herself.

"Thank you for the uh, tip Mr. Parks, but that doesn't sound like anything I would really be interested in. Thank you again though."

She turned and walked away from him quickly. He stood watching her as she rushed away from him in panic while another wicked smile formed on his face. Rachel looked back and saw him, but in her haste, bumped directly into.....

"Oh, I'm....." She gasped as she looked up into his face. Their eyes met and Rachel almost screamed. She managed to hold it in, but covered her mouth just in case. Then she slowly released her mouth and spoke his name.

"Sean!" Her voice was practically a whisper as her eyes grew wide in surprise. She stared at him and tried to regain her composure.

"Rachel! How nice to see you again. Did you come here to see me? Or is there another party going on?" Sean smiled excitedly at her. He was teasing her, but she didn't respond at all like he had hoped she would respond.

"I was just leaving. I came here with co-workers and ..." Rachel did not sound excited to see him at all much to his disappointment.

Sean nodded and held up his hand as if he were hushing her. Rachel stared at him strangely.

"Of course. You have to go now. I understand. I have work to do as well. Maybe we can get together some other time then, Rachel."

Sean sounded disappointed but slowly began to walk away from her. Then he stopped, turned back and walked over to her, as she stood there unwilling to move even though the dancer's occasionally bumped into her. She was getting used to the bodies being so close to her, but she knew there was something more that would not allow her to move. He was making his way toward her again as she watched in silence.

"I can't get in touch with you when I'm free to talk, though can I? I mean, I don't have a number or address where you can be reached. I don't know anything about contacting you, Rachel."

"No, you don't." Rachel said proudly. She wanted to convince him that she was not interested, even if it was not true.

"Oh, I see. You don't want me to contact you. Is that right?"

"No. I don't. I don't want you to contact me. I only came here because of the group. I wouldn't have come here on my own."

"Wow, you are cold, Rachel. I didn't know you were so…."

"I'm just not interested in you, Sean." She said as she looked away from him, but still could not move her feet from that spot. He now stood in front of her and looked her directly in the eyes.

"Not interested? Well, at least you still remember my name. That's a good start." He moved closer to her, held her closely and whispered into her ear. Rachel felt chills running along her spine. She closed her eyes and breathed deeply as he pulled her body close against his. Her heart began to beat rapidly.

"Do you remember what happened Saturday? I keep reliving it over and over again. I would love to feel you naked in my arms right now. You have no idea of how beautiful you are to me, Rachel. I've truly missed you."

Rachel couldn't breathe. She stood there, frozen in terror trying to fight the feelings away. She pushed away from him gently, reluctantly, but didn't go very far. She looked at him again as he moved close to her and took her into his arms again. Sean held her hand then slid his other hand around her waist pulling her close to him. Her body pressed against his as he looked down into her eyes. She couldn't help herself. She felt herself melting in his arms in spite of her reluctance. He held her tightly swaying slowly as the music played loudly. She felt her body give in to him, relaxing as he held her closely. She wrapped her arms around his neck locking her fingers tightly together. Then he unlocked them gently as he spoke to her.

"Come with me, Rachel." He said softly to her. She didn't want to, but she couldn't convince her body to stay put or even to run away. She followed him in spite of everything. She kept her eyes on him as he held her hand and led her away from the crowd again.

This time he took her to the employee's area. No one was there because they were all working. Rachel looked around, but did not protest as he kissed her. She could feel the intensity of desire in his kisses as well as her own. She was no longer fighting against him as he lifted her skirt and lowered her panties. Her back pressed against the locker as she felt him enter her.

"Oh!" she gasped then bit her lip tightly.

"Are you okay?" he asked softly kissing her cheek then neck. When she didn't reply immediately, he looked into her eyes. He wanted to make sure she was okay.

"Yes. I am fine." She replied before he kissed her deeply.

When Rachel got home that night, she fought the urge to cry again. She had cried all the way home in her car, then once she parked, she cried again a few minutes more. She didn't mean to have sex with Sean. Then to add to the hurt and humiliation, she had sex with him in the employee's locker room which made her feel like she had become nothing more than a cheap whore. She was disgusted with herself, ashamed and alone again. She couldn't stop the tears from falling or the aching in her heart.

She felt dirty and wanted to be clean again. She took a hot bath and nearly scrubbed her skin raw. She covered her face and cried again. The anguish she felt was relentless and unending. She could never be clean again from what she had just done. No one would understand, no one. She had given away her body, her holy temple, like a common tramp. She couldn't undo that so she had to live with the shame of her sin.

After her bath, she collapsed on her bed and cried herself to sleep that night, praying hard asking God to cleanse her of her sin, but she didn't receive an answer from Him.

"This time, I know I've done it. God has turned His back on me after He blessed me so greatly today. I turned on Him and gave in to my flesh instead of saying thank you for the blessings. He will never forgive me for this. I may as well just die."

Rachel cried, alone in her apartment until she finally fell asleep.

Confessions

CHERYL composed herself after having a well-deserved cry. Normally she was a strong woman and she intended to remain that way. She rose to her feet and walked over to the wall where she had thrown her phone. She picked it up and looked at it carefully assessing the damage done. The cracked screen was beyond repair.

"Oh great! That is all I need."

She sighed as she looked at the damaged phone for a few more moments.

She walked to the bathroom, cleaned up, got dressed and headed to the nearest cell phone store.

After she purchased a new phone, she went to the senior home and sat with the women for a while. They didn't expect her to visit with them today, but they were more than happy for the company. Cheryl had brought them all boxes of candy, which they all enjoyed. As they sat around talking, giggling and reminiscing, Ms. Stewart looked at Cheryl, who sat there smiling at the women quietly.

"How is everything for the Preacher's loving wife?" asked Ms. Stewart interrupting Cheryl's silence. Cheryl turned to her quickly, as if she were surprised by the question. Ms. Stewart had drawn attention to Cheryl, which is what Cheryl was trying to avoid today.

Ms. Stewart was a wise old woman, small in stature, but pretty sharp as far as people skills. The other women were so busy talking about how they had lived, that none of them took notice of how Cheryl's whole demeanor was different, except Ms. Stewart, but when she questioned her, they immediately focused on Cheryl as well.

Cheryl glanced at Ms. Stewart who immediately searched her face.

"Is everything okay with you, Cheryl? You don't seem like yourself today. You can tell us what's bothering you too, or have you forgotten that this is a *share because we care* group. We all talk about things that are upsetting to us in our lives, and that includes YOU missy. Don't you be holding out on us. We all have been through rough times and we can help you. We'd like to help you for a change."

"There is nothing……" Cheryl began slowly, but Ms. Stewart saw through that story and immediately interrupted her before she could finish.

"Now hold on a minute there. I know you are not about to tell ME that there is nothing wrong! It's written all over your face! Don't even think you can trick me with that bull! I'm not trying to hear it. All I want from you is what you asked us to tell you when we first began doing this….The Truth! You come clean now, or I'm done with this group."

The other women in the group all looked at Cheryl and nodded in agreement with Ms. Stewart.

"You don't want to tell us about your problems?" said one woman.

Then another added, "You think we are too old and senile to understand or help out?"

"No, that's not it at all. Please don't think that way. I'm not saying that. I just ….it's not…" Cheryl fought for the words and in her struggle; tears began to swell in her eyes. She lowered her head to conceal them from the women in the group. Then she spoke softly.

"My marriage isn't as perfect as everyone believes it is. It's hard for me to keep up the image of being a Preacher's wife. Sometimes, I just want to run. Others, I just want to lash out or scream, yet people look to me for guidance. How can I guide anyone when I don't know what to do myself? I'm a failure, my marriage is a failure, and so is my life."

"Well, well now. That's more like it. Those are the words of a real married woman. You wanted us to believe you were an angel or saint or something, but we all know that you are only human. We knew you weren't perfect. None of us are perfect. Why? Because we are made of flesh. Only God is perfect, so to tell yourself that you are perfect is just a lie. People have feelings and that is what God intended. He wants us to have life, but He wants us not to forget what we are living for. God guides you, no, the road is not always easy, but it is His plan for you."

Ms. Stewart spoke gently to Cheryl who sat in silence as the woman continued to speak.

"You do a great job at helping others, Cheryl. That is your gift, but don't forget, God can help you. You just needed to be reminded of that. Whatever it is that you feel is so helpless, or hopeless, God can and will fix."

Cheryl looked at Ms. Stewart and immediately collapsed in the elderly woman's arms. She began to feel better about things. All the other women began to hug her as well.

When Cheryl left the senior home, she felt better. She went home and began to prepare dinner for the night when the house phone rang.

"Hello?" she said.

"Where have you been? I've been waiting for you since 2. You were supposed to be here. You know our time. We've only been seeing each other every day for weeks! Why didn't you show today? What happened? Why did you change the schedule?"

"Matthew, I'm not going to see you anymore. I can't. I'm married and I want my marriage to work. You have to accept that. I'm not doing this anymore. Please don't call here again."

"What? Just like that huh? You think it's that easy? What if I call and talk to your husband? Would you like that? You better think about what you are saying to me. I'll expect you tomorrow, so you better show up or...well, you know what will happen. Oh, why don't you wear some sexy lingerie for me that your husband hasn't seen? I'll be dreaming about you...See you tomorrow, sexy."

Cheryl hung up the phone and fought her tears again.

"Why did I even give in to him the first time." she covered her face, then straightened herself.

"I'll just have to tell Andrew all about it, this way, if he calls back, he won't be doing any damage. Andrew will already hate me and file for a divorce, so there won't be anything he can say to add to it."

Cheryl thought about living her life without Andrew and didn't like the idea at all. She had married him in hopes of the two of them having a good life together, but things hadn't turned out that way. She wanted to have children, but found out later that she couldn't. When she told Andrew that she could not have children, he smiled and told her that they could adopt children when they were ready. He didn't threaten to leave, he never threatened her at all – no matter what. He only showed Cheryl love and deep affection, yet she fell into Matthew's arms so easily.

Cheryl compared the two of them in her mind. Things that Matthew did, helped Cheryl to realize what she had with Andrew. She realized that Andrew was a good man, loving husband and very generous person. She knew that she didn't want to spend her life with anyone else, not even Matthew.

Matthew was better sexually, but that was only because he enjoyed the cunnilingus, something that Andrew felt to be sinful so he had refused to do it for her. That was the only reason she continued to see Matthew, but now, he was threatening to expose her and tell Andrew all about their affair. Suddenly, Cheryl realized that what she was making such a big deal over, didn't matter so much anymore.

Cheryl felt sick to her stomach now. She had wanted to make a dinner for Andrew in an attempt to apologize and try to set things right with him but now, she just felt disgusted with herself again. She turned everything off and went to bed.

When Andrew came in, he saw the pots of unfinished food that Cheryl had begun and sighed.

"She is never going to be able to cook again. I better start eating before I get here." He thought. He got back into his car and drove in search for a nearby restaurant.

"Hmmmm, Spinelli's Spoonful. I guess that's Italian." He chuckled to himself as he parked his car and walked inside.

He ordered his food to go and brought it back to his house where he ate alone, then went to bed.

The next morning, he awakened early and left for work, but forgot to take out the trash in his rush.

Cheryl came down the stairs and quickly spotted the bag from the restaurant.

"Oh my God no!" she screamed. She was terrified. She believed she had lost Andrew forever.

"He knows! He knows about Matthew! He went there to let him know who he is. Oh my God! What am I going to do now? My marriage.....my life...it's finished. Oh, what have I done? I should never have gotten involved with Matthew."

Cheryl felt as if she would explode. She needed to talk to someone, anyone who could help her. She didn't want a divorce, but she was almost certain that Andrew would be filing one very soon. She wanted to talk to someone who would be discrete and be able to offer legal advice.

"Rachel! I will talk to Rachel! She is a legal assistant. She can tell me something."

She rushed to the table, picked up the phone and called Rachel's house....

Truth Shall Set You Free

RACHEL had awakened early and decided to start her first full official day as an attorney immediately. She was determined to put last night's mistake behind her and study her case files to her fullest mental ability. She didn't want to focus on life, or how hers was slowly crumbling apart. She wanted to do everything she could to win her next case.

She jumped out of bed and quickly got ready for work, then rushed to her car. As she rushed out the door, she heard her telephone ring, but decided not to go back and answer it.

"It's probably that guy Sean. I'm not going to talk to him again. I knew I shouldn't have given him my number after we ..." She stopped herself from finishing that statement. She ignored the ringing telephone and got into her car.

When she arrived at work, the assistants that worked in the same area as her smiled and nodded in approval.

"Way to go Rachel!" They all wanted to shake her hand. They were glad that one of their own had earned the title, "Attorney at Law" within the firm.

Rachel was considered a celebrity among them now, but she didn't feel like one. She simply did her job and happened to be in the courtroom while she did it. She was determined to show everyone exactly what she could do and this was her big chance.

When Rachel made her way through the busy office up the stairs to the second level where she took the elevator to her own office on the seventh floor, Violet was standing in front of her door with several messages for her.

"Good morning Violet. How are you doing today?" Rachel said brightly.

"Good morning Attorney…I mean, Rae." Violet said. Rachel nodded approvingly.

"Very good. You remembered. Are all those messages for me? I just started yesterday." Rachel was joking, but Violet began to rummage through them checking information.

"Violet, I'm kidding. I'll take them. Please relax a little you are making me very nervous." Rachel said as she walked into her office.

"Mr. Knight called last night after you left with the other attorneys. He wanted to know what is happening with his case now that Faye Burton is not representing him. Mr. Mitchell's secretary recommended that he talk to you and you could explain that you are representing him. Well, he was the first one that called. All of your messages are from clients that are debating on whether or not they want to continue with the firm or go to another now that Faye is no longer representing them."

Rachel's spirits began to dampen, but she shielded this from Violet.

"Thank you Violet. I will call them and explain what has happened."

"That is a very good idea, Rae. I know they will like you once they talk to you. You are just a naturally pleasant person. They will like you much better than Faye for sure." Violet stated then turned and walked back to her desk. Rachel slowly closed the door to her office and sat at her desk exhausted already and her day was just beginning.

"Oh my Lord, if I lose these clients, my employment here is history. Give me the wisdom necessary and the words that I need to say to these clients, please."

After saying her prayer, she took a deep breath and began to return the worried clientele's calls.

"Hello, Mr. Knight. My name is Rachel Jensen and I am the attorney representing you now that Ms. Burton is no longer with our firm."

"You are? How did you get my case? What happened to Faye? What's going on there?" Mr. Knight questioned rapidly.

Mr. Knight was suing a company that he worked for because he was injured on the job. His case was to be heard within the next few days, so she wanted to talk to him first. She knew she had to calm him down

"I acquired your case as an assistant to Faye, so I can assure you that no one knows your case better than I do. I realize also that you may not feel comfortable with me. I understand that but the thing is ...this. It will take months to get back to this point in your case. If you want this case done quickly then I'm the counsel for the job. We will win this case. However, you do have the option of seeking other counsel instead. The final decision is yours, Mr. Knight. Do you want to win, or wait?"

"Ms. Jensen, you make a very good point there. Besides, all the money that I've spent on this case is breaking me. You've studied my case and you believe it can be won?"

"Yes sir Mr. Knight. I most definitely do."

"Then why was Faye telling me that I needed to postpone the court dates and draw it out like that?"

"I really couldn't say, Mr. Knight. I'm sure that whatever her reasons were, she did what she thought was right but I CAN tell you that we WILL win this case."

"So, the firm has been swindling me? What the…"

"Mr. Knight, I must apologize, but that is not necessarily true. Faye was in charge of your case, not the firm. Only she and I had access to your files. I was just an assistant so I was not allowed to tell an attorney what to do in regard to the cases. However, I'm telling you now because I am your attorney now. We can win this case. We will win or you will not have to pay anything at all."

Mr. Knight began to relax.

"So are you going to make the same fee that Faye did?"

"I'm afraid so, but it is mostly for the firm's staff. I will get a portion, but the assistants get an hourly wage, so a majority of the money paid to the firm will go to them."

"You know your stuff don't you, Rachel. I like that. You have convinced me. I will allow you to handle my case, but remember what you said. You said you can win. That is what I expect. No more delays. I want it done and over with. Understand?"

"Yes, Sir. I understand and don't worry. I will definitely finish it. You will be very happy with the results, Mr. Knight. Thank you for allowing me to be your lawyer."

"You are welcome, Ms. Jensen. Just keep your word and don't make me regret it."

Mr. Knight hung up the phone then Rachel did the same.

"One down, nine more to go." She sighed as she began to dial the next phone number.

When Rachel was done making calls to her clientele, she was exhausted. She hadn't had lunch yet and it was late afternoon. She needed to take a well-deserved break. She stood up and stretched as she walked over to the window and looked out at the street below the seven-story high office view. She wasn't afraid of heights, but was beginning to be thankful that her office wasn't any higher the longer she looked down.

"Wow. It is all so overwhelming. God is good." Rachel said to herself, "But I am such a terrible sinner." She closed her eyes and fought her tears again. She blinked hard and quickly wiped her eyes before the tears could escape. She took a deep breath and sat at her desk again. She wanted to get something to eat now. She knew Violet wasn't allowed to have lunch at the same time as her because her phones would not be covered if they both had lunch together so she decided to order from a nearby restaurant so that they both could enjoy lunch.

She had plenty of room in her office, so she decided to do that.

"Violet, would you like to have lunch?" Rachel asked.

"Oh, I'd love to, but who will cover the phones?"

"We can have our lunch here. Where should we order from?"

Violet made the call for the food delivery and Rachel paid for it. While they were having lunch in her office, Russell Parks stopped by Rachel's office.

"Well hello there, Attorney. Looking sharp today. You're going to fit in here nicely. I have to admit that I was skeptical last night, but now, I'm sure you are just another one of the guys."

Rachel didn't like talking to him. She looked at Violet who also sighed in frustration as Russell continued to annoy them.

"Speaking of last night, we are going to head back to that little club later tonight. Would you like to come along?"

Rachel immediately shook her head.

"No, thank you. I have made other plans but thank you anyway for the offer."

Russell smiled politely.

"Oh, I see. You just wanted to catch up with your old friend, the bartender huh? Where did you two run off to so quickly, anyway? You looked like you were truly in love." Russell smiled as terror began to surge through Rachel's body. She hadn't realized that he had seen her with Sean. She didn't know what to say. Violet looked at her and knew she was taken off guard.

"Mr. Parks, we are having lunch now. Please come back and visit in an hour for a full consultation."

Violet walked over to the door and closed it gently as Russell walked away laughing loudly.

Rachel was no longer hungry. She couldn't think straight or even talk now. She wanted to cry. She wanted to be forgiven. She wanted to forget last night. She wanted to be clean again, but she felt like she never would be clean again. Violet touched her shoulder gently.

"Rae? Do you want to talk about something?" she asked.

Rachel shook her head.

"No, please, Violet, enjoy your lunch. Don't mind me. I'm fine."

Both she and Violet knew that was not true. Violet simply looked at her.

"Alright, I'm not fine, but don't worry. I will be. I just need some time to figure a few things out. It's nothing that can't be fixed."

"That man is a major jerk. I heard that he had an assistant before who was trying to earn her stripes and graduate to the level of attorney here. The rumor was he told her that he would help her if she uh…did certain favors for him in return. She allegedly did and he didn't lift a finger to help her out. In fact, the rumor says that he got her fired after she slept with him. He told the board that they had sex, but he told them it was her who suggested it and he was just an innocent victim of her charms. She used him to try to advance in her career."

"Good grief! That is not fair at all. I knew this firm did not stand up for the assistants, but I had no idea that it had been that dramatic."

Rachel thought about how Russell had looked at her last night. She shook her head to remove the image of his wicked smile from her mind.

"He isn't a very nice man that is obvious. I also believe that he would do anything he can to destroy his competition. I am hoping that I am wrong about that, but he is the top attorney for a reason. Faye is probably the only one who could have given him a run for his money, but now she is gone. He may think I did him a favor by being a part of her reason for departure from the firm. Why else would he want to celebrate with everyone and then.....make a pass at me?"

Rachel hadn't meant to say that last part aloud but had thought it. When she did, she immediately gasped and covered her mouth quickly. She turned to see if Violet had heard her but Violet's eyes were already wide as she stared at her.

"What? He made a pass at you? That's harassment! You could use that against him, Rae. You are the attorney here, I don't have to tell you that, I'm sure."

Violet spoke as if she wanted to get even with Russell for something. Rae looked at her and wondered what he had done to her, but hesitated to ask.

"Right, I guess I could, but what would be the point of that? He is beneficial to this firm, just as the other attorneys are. He has the top paying clients and wins the biggest cases for the firm. I don't think it's necessary to charge him with something so miniscule. It wasn't that dramatic. It was just a simple little misunderstanding. That's all."

"Rae, I can't believe that you don't want to threaten him or press charges against him. What kind of a woman are you? Don't you know a chauvinistic pig when you see one? He is a real piece of..."

Rachel immediately interrupted Violet.

"Violet! Please, I don't want to talk about it anymore. I didn't think it was that big of a deal. I'm not going to try to blow it way out of proportion unless I feel it is necessary later on. However, you seem like you have a lot of animosity toward Russell. Would you like to talk to me and tell me why?"

Violet rose to her feet and sighed deeply.

"No. I'm not talking about it anymore either. Russell Parks is a jerk and someday, he will get exactly what is coming to him."

Violet began to clean up the lunch table silently as Rachel watched her. Violet was her only friend in the world right now, she could not afford to lose her. She had to say something to her and calm her.

"I'm sorry if I've made you angry, Violet. Perhaps I shouldn't toss the idea of pressing charges against him completely, but maybe if you told me why you hate him so much, we could both press charges against him. If he is such a jerk to you, you can trust me to help you get rid of him."

Violet huffed loudly.

"Spoken like a true attorney. If I let my guard down and trust you, then you take out the dagger and stab me in the back with it. I should know better."

"Violet, I wouldn't do anything like that to you. You are my friend. I'm just trying to figure out what is right here. I'm not out to get you at all. Please don't think that way. I am an attorney, but I'm not like the ones you know. I try to find all the facts before I make a decision, just as a normal person would. That's all. Don't be angry. I couldn't...."

Rachel walked over to the window. She couldn't talk anymore. She felt as if the world were turning on her again. She took a deep breath as Violet stared at her.

"Rae, I'm sorry. I shouldn't have gotten angry because you won't help me to get revenge on him. He is my problem and not yours. I understand. I was wrong to try to pressure you into doing something you don't want to do. I hope you don't fire me for talking to you like that. It's just that he gets away with causing so much trouble... I just can't stand him."

"Don't worry Violet. He causes trouble, but he will eventually answer for all the things he has done. It's not necessarily our place to judge him. Just take things as they come and be patient. He will have to face up to the problems he has caused for others someday."

"You are way too calm with that stuff. If it were me, I'd be going to the police right now. I'm sure the board would offer me a huge settlement. One so large that I would never have to work again! However, I enjoy working...especially with you Rae. You are definitely different. You are one of the sweetest people I've ever met. Thank you for lunch."

Violet threw out the trash, then returned to her desk. She didn't seem as angry as she was before. Rachel felt calm herself now. She hadn't lost Violet's friendship but she had failed to maintain her relationship with her own sister.

"The truth shall set you free..." she thought again as she sat at her desk and reviewed the files.

Revelations

RACHEL tried hard to concentrate on the files, but she kept drifting back to what happened with Sean. She could feel his touch, taste his kiss and hear his voice as he spoke to her soothingly.

"You feel so good Rachel." He breathed into her ear as they had sex.

Rachel shook her head slightly, rested her elbows upon her desk, and then rested her head upon her hands as if they were holding her head up. She wanted to concentrate on work, but she continued to struggle.

She began to see the faces of the congregation all staring at her and pointing fingers.

"Jezebel!

Harlot!

Sleazy whore!

Tramp!" They all called her names as they pointed their fingers in anger at her. She began to plead her case.

"It was an accident. I didn't mean for it to happen. I'm not those terrible things. I'm a child of God. Why can't you forgive me? I meant no harm."

"You have sinned in the eyes of The Lord! You are not worthy of being His child! You shall be removed from the church, forever! God has not forgiven you, Harlot! Get your sinful flesh out of this holy place!"

Rachel was near tears from thoughts of what the congregation would say if they knew about her and Sean when Violet knocked on her door.

"Rae, you have a phone call. I've been trying to buzz you, but you didn't respond. Do you have a headache? I can get you something for it if you like."

Rachel blinked her eyes and strategically wiped the tears. Violet didn't notice even though she stared at her. Rachel put forth her best smile as she spoke to Violet.

"Thank you Violet. I'm okay. I don't really have a headache, but was just concentrating on my file. I do appreciate your concern though. Do you have any idea of who it is that is calling for me?"

"Oh, I'm sorry. Yes, she said her name was Cheryl Montgomery. She said she really needs to speak to you.

She said it is a private matter, but of the utmost importance." Violet said.

Rachel immediately began to panic.

"How did she find out? What do I do? Oh no! They are going to kick me out of church and brand me as a whore." She thought as she fought to control the terror building up inside of her.

"Thank you Violet. Please, put the call through." Rachel's voice quivered slightly as she continued to fight for control.

Violet nodded then returned to her desk.

"Please hold Ms. Montgomery, I am transferring your call right now."

"Thank you."

Cheryl was a nervous wreck. She didn't know where to begin the conversation with Rachel, but she knew that talking over the telephone was not a good idea. They had to meet in person to discuss this and Cheryl was not going to accept no for an answer from Rachel.

"Hello Mrs. Montgomery." Rachel began politely.

"Hello Rachel. I know you are probably busy, but it is very important that I speak with you. I need to talk to you, but not over the telephone. This matter is very personal and very private. I need you to meet me someplace as soon as possible."

Rachel's panic began to grow.

"What exactly is this about…" Rachel began, but Cheryl cut her off.

"Rachel, I do not want to discuss it over the phone. In person, okay? I'll explain everything when I see you. You can decide where we meet if you want, but it has to be in person and it has to be today! The sooner the better."

Rachel took a deep breath.

"If she knows about it, the entire congregation knows. Either she is trying to keep me from returning to church and being embarrassed, or she is setting me up for it. She probably knew something when she saw me on Sunday, but now…."

Rachel thought logically about what she was telling herself.

"How could she know? I didn't see anyone watching us. If she was there…. No, she couldn't have been there. Why would such a true woman of God go to such a place? She must know someone who was there and they told her." Rachel's panicked thoughts continued to flood her mind.

"Okay, since you don't have any place in mind to meet me, I will tell you were we can meet. I will meet you at your place. What time are you leaving work?"

"I uh….I usually leave…any time after five, but I can't meet you today. I am sorry, but I have several cases that must be reviewed first. I cannot neglect my clients." Rachel hesitated before answering, but Cheryl was on a mission. She needed to talk to her and soon.

"Alright. I will meet you at your place at 5:30 tomorrow. As I said before, it is a matter of the utmost importance and discretion."

"Alright Mrs. Cheryl. I will try to be on time. I will talk to you then, and don't worry. I won't say anything about our meeting to anyone." Rachel said.

"Good. I will talk to you tomorrow then Rachel. Have a good evening."

"You too, Mrs. Cheryl. Good bye." Rachel said as she slowly replaced the receiver of the phone to the base.

Cheryl began to wonder why Rachel was so hesitant to talk to her as she hung up the phone slowly.

"Did Andrew already consult with Rachel for legal advice? She probably knows everything and doesn't want to talk to me because she thinks I…"

Cheryl took a deep breath. She didn't want to finish that thought. If everyone at the church knew about her affair with Matthew, they would no longer look up to her. They would dessert her and call her all kinds of names. They would say that she is a slut who is not worthy of Andrew at all even though she loved him and is willing to work things out.

Cheryl had to find out what Andrew told Rachel, then explain her side of the story. Rachel was going to have to be the intermediary in their divorce battle. Cheryl was not going to give up Andrew without a fight. She knew that without him, she would be even more miserable.

Rachel hung up the phone slowly. She did not want to talk to Cheryl today because she knew she would not be able to handle any more stress. She began to dread the upcoming meeting. She looked at her files and tried to concentrate again, but failed miserably. She only thought of last night with Sean and meeting with Cheryl. She wasn't able to accomplish much work by five, so she called it a day and headed toward home, reluctantly.

Forgiveness Doesn't Come Easy

RACHEL drove by the park where she spotted children playing happily. She decided to visit for a while, so she parked her car and slowly made her way to a nearby bench where she watched the children playing. She remembered how she and Frances used to play when they were children. Everything was so innocent and carefree. She wished they were children again. She missed being able to talk to Frances. Then she began to think about Sean.

She began to remember how she felt when she was with him. He told her that she was beautiful as he touched her body. She remembered how warm his hands felt against her skin as she welcomed him inside of her body. She remembered how she trembled in his arms. He had asked her if he could see her again and she did not deny him this. She had given him her telephone number, but decided not to give him anything more. She planned to be at work when he called her so she would not have to talk to him.

Rachel hoped that she would be able to avoid Sean's calls by working late and going to sleep early. Then again, she wasn't even sure if he would call her. She began to think that he was just being polite when he asked her if he could see her again sometime once they had sex. She had given him what he wanted like a common whore, so what reason would he have to possibly call her now? She couldn't think of anything.

A man selling ice cream slowly strolled by her. The children playing all surrounded him eagerly. She watched them as they scraped up their money in attempts to purchase some of the frosty treats that were for sale. Rachel rose to her feet and made her way through the crowd of children. Some of them had money to buy treats, but a few did not. They looked so sad. Rachel hated seeing the children look so sad. She called out to the man and spoke above the excited children.

"How much is it for each child to have an ice cream bar?" She asked immediately getting everyone's attention. The man raised an eyebrow at her strangely, but all the children were thankful.

"Gee! Thanks lady!" "Wow! Thanks a million lady!" the children all thanked her excitedly once they picked out their ice cream, received it and walked away to eat it. Rachel smiled and some even took the liberty of hugging her. She remembered when she was a child and how she had felt when she wanted ice cream, but had no money. She knew how the children felt.

Once everyone had an ice cream bar, Rachel watched the children happily eating their treats as she paid the man for them.

"You must be pretty rich there lady to spend so much money on a bunch of kids you don't know." The man said as he collected the money.

Rachel shook her head.

"I wouldn't say I was rich financially, but I have been blessed. Therefore, I must share my blessing with those who are less fortunate. Look at those happy faces. Children are truly gifts from God. They are so wonderful to watch, to talk to and I just adore them."

"You don't have any, do you? I think that is why you like them so much. Most parents would not agree with you, but hey, that's not my business. I thank you for the purchases though. Thanks a lot."

The man began to push the ice cream cart away from the area as Rachel turned and waved good bye to the happy children. They all waved back at her eagerly saying thank you again. She made her way to her car and drove home.

When Rachel opened the door to her apartment, she heard the dial tone buzzing from her answering machine. She had just missed a phone call. She rushed to it to listen to the message, but it was blank. She thought it might be Frances who changed her mind and decided to continue being angry with her.

"Frances, why didn't you leave a message? Are you going to hate me forever?"

Rachel closed her eyes and lowered her head as if she were truly defeated. She wanted Frances to talk to her, but something told her that she would not give in to Rachel. She sighed deeply then prepared herself for bed. Thoughts of meeting with Cheryl tomorrow began to come back to her as she lay in bed staring helplessly at the ceiling in her dark bedroom. She wanted to relax, but she was very much on edge about it. She wanted to think of an explanation for what she had done, but she couldn't think clearly.

"Why should I try to lie to her, she isn't stupid. She saw something when we were at church. I may as well confess the whole thing to her. She has to know already, somehow. That is why she called me at work. It is important that I volunteer and confess my sins before the others find out and begin to penalize me for my mistake. I didn't think that being a single Christian was....well, I never thought it would be like this. I know I should have waited for the right man and gotten married, but I felt so alone. I couldn't help myself, it happened so quickly. Everything was happening just so… Was I wrong to do it? My body didn't even struggle against it, but…Oh God, forgive me, please!"

Rachel felt very ashamed as she lay there in bed. She closed her eyes, pleading for forgiveness mentally, blaming herself for giving in to the temptations of her unclean body and not seeking God before making such a mess of things. She felt hopeless, helpless and alone. Her loneliness seemed to haunt her relentlessly. She tossed and turned most of the night, trying not to think about anything until she thought of Sean again. She wrapped her arms around herself tightly.

"No, please, no more." She whispered, but she was no longer in control of herself. Her body began to react as if he were there with her. She sighed and moaned as she fought to control herself but failed. Sean gave her an orgasm without even being there ……for the second time. Rachel was finally exhausted enough to fall asleep now.

In God's Hands

CHERYL left her house after talking with Rachel. She wanted to run a few errands and thought about Rachel as she got into her car and began to drive

"Rachel knows something, she has to know something. Her reaction was a dead giveaway. She is hiding something, I know she is, but what is she...going to do with the information she has?"

Cheryl was going to find out one way or another. She was determined and knew that she would not be able to rest peacefully until she did know exactly what Rachel had been told. She had to prepare herself mentally for the meeting with Rachel. She had scheduled it without giving it much thought. She simply wanted to talk to her and have the opportunity to explain her side of the story.

Cheryl had wanted to tell Matthew that it was over and that she was no longer going to see him, so she went to the restaurant where he worked.

Matthew was glad to see her at first, but that quickly changed. She motioned for him to meet her outside, which he did as soon as he could. Cheryl stood with her back against the door of her car as he called out to her.

"Hi there sexy! I'm glad you came to see me today. I thought I was going to have to call your house again."

Matthew spoke happily as he approached her practically running. Cheryl held up her hand immediately stopping him from hugging her.

"Matthew, listen to me! I'm not here to arrange another meeting. In fact, I came to tell you that I don't want to see you anymore. It's time for us to let this thing go."

They stood there in silence for a few moments. Matthew looked at her questioningly, so she repeated herself.

"I'm not going to see you anymore. I am staying with my husband and there is nothing that you can do or say to stop me. He and I are going to work this mistake out and save our marriage."

Matthew looked at her in silence as she spoke to him. She seemed so sincere and determined, but he still appeared to be confused about what she was saying. After a few moments, he turned and slowly walked back toward the restaurant. She watched him in silence then he turned toward her, clapped his hands and scoffed.

"Very good! Now, say it once more with feeling. I want to really believe the words that I just heard. You are quite the actress, Cheryl. You actually managed to convince me for a minute, but only for a minute. Do you honestly believe that your husband will forgive you for sleeping with me all this time? I don't think you have a chance in hell at saving your marriage, but if you feel you do, my advice would be....Go for it! Besides, you need his money to buy me that leather jacket I wanted and some more sexy lingerie too.

Matthew quickly snatched her into his arms pressing his body into hers in spite of her struggling.

"Let go of me, Matthew!" Cheryl said annoyed. She tossed her head from side to side to avoid eye contact with him as he held her.

"It's okay, sweetness. I'm not trying to make a scene here, just wanted you to feel what you do to me."

He continued to press his body against hers as he slowly rocked back and forth. She looked at him and felt his manhood pressed against her. He smiled down at her as she stared at him in silence unable to move. He always knew how to get to her. She hated herself for being so weak with him. She had enjoyed every interlude they had experienced together, but she knew in her heart that she loved Andrew. Matthew lowered his head and kissed her cheek gently as she closed her eyes and submitted to him.

"Good God woman I want you so bad right now." he whispered into her ear. She wanted to fling her arms around his neck and allow him to take her right there, but managed to push away from him. She breathed hard and blinked as she attempted to regain her composure.

Matthew stepped backward, smiling wickedly at her, then spoke.

"I'll see you later at the usual place baby. Daddy's gonna spank ya later, but I've gotta get back to work, so I can't play with you right now." He spoke smugly then blew her a kiss as she stared in silence.

Then Matthew spoke softly as he turned and walked back toward the restaurant.

"I'm glad you want our relationship to go public because, that's what I want too. No more secret mess. It will be so much better!"

Matthew continued to walk away from Cheryl, but looked back at her and waved. She stared at him as the last words echoed in her mind.

"Oh my God." Cheryl opened the door to her car slowly. Her fears began to consume her. Matthew didn't seem worried at all while she couldn't stop trembling from the thoughts of Andrew possibly knowing.

"Perhaps, Andrew did go to the restaurant last night to confront him about the affair, but why would Matthew keep that a secret from me? What have I done? Can my marriage be saved? Will Andrew ever forgive me for what I did? Do I even deserve his ... or anyone's forgiveness?"

Cheryl fought her tears again as more and more questions danced around inside of her head causing her to continue to lose hope of saving her life together with Andrew. She realized that she had made a terrible mistake and would pay the price for it.

She knew that she could not face Andrew. The guilt she was feeling was much too great to allow it. Matthew had wanted her to stay the night with him before, but she never did because of Andrew. Now, she didn't know if she should just give in to that or not. She felt so confused. Her heart felt as if it were in the middle of a tremendous tug of war and it was going to break no matter what the outcome was.

Cheryl drove around the city for hours aimlessly. She wanted to do something nice for Andrew, but she was convinced that he already hated her. She felt useless, unloved and hurt. She turned away from the only man that ever truly loved her and in turn, hurt him so badly that he could never possibly love her again.

She made her way back home and parked her car. She didn't bother with making dinner because she felt so empty, that nothing mattered to her anymore. She didn't want anything now. She even thought that she shouldn't be allowed to live, but she knew that was God's decision and not hers. The anguish made it hard for her to move physically, but she managed to get into bed where she cried herself to sleep that night.

Andrew worked late that night again because he did not want to argue with Cheryl. He knew that when she was ready to talk to him, that she would, but so far, she hadn't even been trying to see him. This argument had definitely been one of their worst, but like the other ones they had, they would also get through this one by the grace of God.

The house seemed to be so much larger than when they first moved there now because of Cheryl's constant efforts to avoid him. He sighed as he made his way to the guest bedroom again and prepared for bed.

Andrew hated sleeping there, but he knew Cheryl was not ready to talk to him. He was determined to let her work through whatever it was that was bothering her. He believed that she was so distant because she had found someone else, but then he thought better. Cheryl loved him that is why she married him. She could have had any man she wanted, but she chose him. He was foolish for thinking that she would betray him so shamefully. He knew he had jumped to the wrong conclusion and began to relax again.

He had blamed himself for the argument as well, so he knew it wasn't all her fault. He said things that she didn't agree with, but he still loved her greatly. He simply wanted to let her know his viewpoint on the issue and did not mean to make her feel like a tramp or anything. He told her that as well, but she still blamed herself for not being able to have children, so she may feel the same way about this argument as well.

Andrew thought about going to her and making sure that she knew he knew she was not a tramp. He also wanted her to know that he still loved her, but decided against it because he would be intruding upon the time she needed to think. He shook his head and laughed to himself when he thought about the possibility of Cheryl having an affair.

"Cheryl would never do something like that. She is my wife and yeah, we argue, but deep down, we are still in love. She isn't that kind of woman."

He felt silly for thinking that she would do such a thing to him now. He trusted her completely and began to believe that if she said that she was trying to help someone, then that is exactly what she was doing. She didn't need to lie to him about anything, so why would she lie about trying to help a homeless man?

"I should have known better than that. When she talks to me, I will confess that I thought she had done something terrible and we will both have a fantastic laugh at my expense of course, but seeing her laugh will make it all better."

Andrew shook his head, laughed softly and fell asleep.

The next morning, he got up and got ready for work as usual while Cheryl slept late. The avoidance continued much to Andrew's disappointment. He truly missed having his wife next to him at night and sending him off to work the next day. He began to wonder if he would ever have her back. He peeked into the room while she was asleep and watched her for a moment. She looked so beautiful lying there. He wanted to kiss her and tell her that everything was going to be all right. He made his way over to her slowly and kissed her delicately as she slept.

"I love you, Cheryl. I always will. Please don't forget that." He whispered to her after he kissed her. She stirred but did not awaken. Andrew could tell that she had been crying and his heart sank. He wanted to be able to console her and cheer her up no matter what she was going through, but she would never tell him what it was. He felt helpless as he slowly straightened his body and made his way out of the room.

"It's all in God's hands and he is more than capable of delivering her from whatever she is facing. I just have to be patient." He said to himself as he made his way to the front door.

The Awakening

CHERYL awakened and then began her day. She was interrupted during her shower by the sound of her telephone ringing. She was breathing rapidly as she reached for the telephone that rested on the stand next to her bed. She sat on the bed quickly and looked around.

"Hello?" Cheryl said quickly into the receiver.

"Hi there Sweets. I missed you yesterday. Hell, I missed you a lot! What happened? Did the rev keep you from visiting with me?"

"You are not supposed to call me here! Stop it! I know you aren't this stupid! You can't be. Well…" Cheryl said angrily but Matthew interrupted her scoffing loudly at her insult.

"I know, but you won't answer me anywhere else. I have to call you. Didn't you hear me say I missed you? What did you think I was joking? I'm serious! I want to see you. I want … No, I need to see you now! It's urgent! No more games because that crap is just too damned annoying." Matthew sounded irritated, but was far from angry with her. Cheryl shook her head and began to speak again.

"I told you…." Cheryl began, but Matthew quickly interrupted her again. He was irritated with her excuses.

"I heard you when you said that garbage yesterday and I'm still not convinced. You want to convince me that you are done with me, then this is how you do it. Come to the door, let me in and prove it to me physically!"

"What?"

Cheryl got off the bed and looked out the window. Matthew was standing there looking up at her window.

"Go home! You can't come here!" Cheryl said into the phone.

"Why not? I told you I want to see you. You think I'm kidding? Well, I'm serious. I say what I mean, unlike you."

Cheryl was terrified. She had no idea of whether or not Andrew had already left for work. She breathed hard. Her pulse rate increased and she wrapped her free arm around herself in an effort to calm down. She had even forgotten that she was only wearing a towel. She opened the door to her bedroom slowly searched the house and eventually made her way to the kitchen. She didn't see any signs of Andrew. She began to calm down again.

She walked to the front door where Matthew was waiting. She took a deep breath before opening it slowly.

"I really wish you hadn't come here, Matthew. Please leave now." Cheryl said as she stood there, peeking from the small opening. She attempted to shield herself when she realized that she was not dressed. Matthew's reaction to her made her remember this.

"I see you are dressed for the occasion. I like it a lot. I'd love to see it on the floor though. Come here sexy. I've been waiting to get my hands on you for a long time now. Don't disappoint me now." Matthew reached for her hungrily as she gasped and stepped backward releasing the door.

"Oh no." She thought as he smiled and walked into the house slowly closing the door behind him.

Matthew walked toward her smiling wickedly. Cheryl wanted to run, but stood there.

"Matthew, you need to leave. I cannot do this. I cannot do this again." She said as he wrapped his arms around her.

"It's okay. I'll take care of you. Just relax." He whispered into her ear as he kissed her neck. Cheryl immediately began to grow weak in his arms. She fought her tears as he kissed her hungrily pressing his body to hers.

"I've waited so long....too long to have you, Cheryl." Matthew said before kissing her deeply. Cheryl couldn't resist him now no matter how hard she wanted to.

"Forgive me, Andrew."

She thought as Matthew lifted her into his arms and lay her on the floor gently. He smiled at her as he knelt above her, then removed his shirt quickly before kissing her again.

Cheryl stared at the ceiling as she felt his hands and lips gliding slowly along her now exposed skin exploring her sensually. She didn't remember him removing his pants, but he had done so because she felt his skin between her thighs. She closed her eyes, gasping softly and surrendered her body to Matthew yet again.

"That's my good girl. Mmmm, you're a very good girl, aren't you Cheryl." Matthew said as he returned his lips to hers kissing her deeply.

Apologies

RACHEL decided to call Frances before she went to work. She dialed her number and waited for her to answer, but she did not. Rachel was quite certain that it was Frances who had called her earlier so she decided to see where Frances was calling from by looking at the caller ID. The number listed on the caller ID was not familiar so she decided to try to reach Frances there. She soon found out that she was not calling Frances at all.

"Hello?" said a familiar voice. Rachel gasped in spite of herself because she quickly recognized the voice of Sean.

"He called me?" Rachel thought as she held the phone to her ear and tried to hold her breath.

"Rachel? Is that you?" said Sean. Rachel was paralyzed in fear. She couldn't move, or breathe. She just held the receiver tightly in her grasp.

"What's wrong? Are you okay? Do you need me to come over? Rachel, answer me?" Sean sounded desperate now. Rachel had to calm him down or she would be in trouble again.

"I'm sorry. I was getting ready for work and dialed your number unknowingly. You are the last person who called me apparently. Sorry I bothered you so early." Rachel said apologetically.

She was truly sorry that she had dialed the number now, but she could tell that Sean was glad to hear from her. She didn't want to make herself appear desperate, but deep down, she was glad to hear from him as well. She also knew she would never admit it to him though.

"Well, I'm glad you called me back. I was beginning to feel used for a bit there. I wouldn't do that to you, though Rachel. It's always good to hear from you, even if it was an honest mistake. I don't mind. I'll take what I can get with you." Sean was teasing her, but Rachel didn't think it was funny.

"Oh, really? Do you think I'm some kind of a joke or something? Well, it was a mistake and see if ......" Rachel said in an attempt to shield her surging anger. Sean immediately responded interrupting her.

"No that's not...Rachel, now hold on there. I don't think you are a joke, not at all. Don't get angry with me. I was simply trying to lighten the mood. You are so serious all the time, Rachel. I just wanted to make you laugh a little. I guess I suck huh? Sorry about that. I could never think of YOU as a joke, Rachel. I thought you knew that about me. I guess I didn't make that clear either."

They were both silent for a while. Rachel didn't know how to carry on the conversation now that she had accused him of being a jerk. Sean wasn't willing to give up though.

"Okay, no more bad jokes. It's way too early anyway. So, what time do you get off work?" Sean asked continuing the conversation and ending the awkward silence.

"I usually work until about 5, but I have a meeting at 5:30 today, so I'm not sure when I will be done with work officially today at least." Rachel said. Sean sighed loudly.

"It's hard to catch you alone isn't it Rachel. I gotta admit, you are giving me a run for my money, but ...I also have to admit that you are so worth it. I'd really like to see you sometime soon."

Sean paused for a moment then continued.

"I tell you what. I'll call you later on tonight. If you are free, we can do something, but if not, I'll try again tomorrow. How does that sound to you? Better yet, do you have any plans for tomorrow?"

Rachel's eyes grew wide in fear. She did not want to go out with Sean. She knew it would only lead to more trouble for her. She quickly covered her mouth to try and think of a way to get rid of him politely. Then he spoke.

"Be honest and don't make stuff up just to avoid me, okay? I know you are probably trying to do that. Why don't you want to go out with me Rachel?"

Sean asked sounding clearly confused. Rachel looked at the receiver as if he could see the look on her face. She shook her head and scoffed silently. "I may as well be honest. No use in lying to him. It's not right and he can tell if I did lie to him anyway." She thought as she slowly returned the receiver to her ear.

"I don't have plans yet, but…"

"Great! I'll take you out tomorrow! Let's see. You get off at five…Oh nuts! I have to be at work. I work nights. Can you come to the club tomorrow night?"

"No! I can't! I'm not going back there." Rachel said annoyed. Sean immediately apologized even though he didn't really know why she didn't want to go back to the club.

"Alright. It's okay. I'm sorry. Don't be angry, it was just a thought. I just really want to see you that's all. That was stupid. I shouldn't have asked you to come to my job anyway. Do you think you could forgive me?"

Rachel's eyes were wide. Those words stayed with her for a moment. She looked down at the phone, then slowly lifted her head. She couldn't stop thinking about those words. She repeated them.

"Forgive you?"

She looked around the room and spotted her reflection in the mirror as she spoke to Sean. She couldn't help saying the words again.

"Forgive you?" she said softly again. "Of course. You haven't done anything wrong. There is nothing to forgive."

Rachel began to think about the words she just said. She looked at the telephone again, but continued to think. Suddenly she had an unusual thought.

"Maybe that is what God is trying to tell me?" she thought. She didn't see how God could forgive her for acting like a cheap whore, but she did know that HE had always looked beyond her faults before. Why couldn't He do it again? Had He already forgiven her for being less than perfect? Questions continued to arise in her mind as Sean began to speak again. His voice brought her back to reality.

"Well, good. I wouldn't want you to be angry with me when I just want to see you. You are pretty difficult though. I've always liked that about you. Well, I know you have to get ready for work, so I won't take up too much time. You have my number now, so you can call me, but I'll probably be doing all the calling. I don't mind though. So, I will talk to you later and see you tomorrow. Don't worry, I'll call you before I just show up. I have to because I don't have your address yet. Do you want to go out with me tomorrow?" Sean waited for Rachel's response barely breathing.

"I...uh...I...well. I don't know. I will let you know later. I may have an important meeting. These things happen and I'm not really in control of my schedule anymore. I've got cases and trials. It's a lot...."

"Cases? Trials? You are an attorney?" Sean asked

"Yes. I am. I was recently..." Rachel began, but Sean interrupted excitedly.

"Wow! I didn't even know. That's fantastic, Rachel! Congratulations! No wonder you are so busy. I see now. You aren't just blowing me off."

Rachel laughed as she shook her head. Sean heard her and immediately laughed along.

"Oh, so you think that one is funny huh? Wait till we have our date tomorrow, I'll crack you up now that I know what you like." Sean was teasing her again. Rachel couldn't help the smile that formed on her face, but she had to get ready for work.

"Well, good luck Sean. It's not easy to make me laugh, especially now, but I really have to go. It's been nice talking to you. Bye now."

"Bye bye now, Rachel. Thanks for accidentally calling me. It was the best accident I'll have all day, I'm sure. Talk to you later. Have a great day at work. Miss you already." Sean said as he slowly hung up his phone. Rachel slowly lowered her phone as well but looked at it strangely as she did.

"Miss you?" She thought about what he had said to her. She had been in a relationship before, but he never told her that he missed her. Was this one going to be different from the mistake she made before or was she reading too much into it, forcing herself to have feelings that weren't there or genuine.

"Sean misses me? Why would he say that? This has to be a joke. Why would he miss me?" Rachel felt happy for a moment, but it quickly faded away. The longer she thought about it, the less she believed it to be true.

"He just wants more sex from me. He doesn't miss me or even care about me. He just wants to use my body for his pleasure and he wants me to go along with it willingly. I have to stop tricking myself into believing

that someone…Oh, never mind. Just get to work Rachel!"
She told herself quickly growing frustrated with the
whole situation again.

Rachel drove to work as quickly as she could and
immediately began to submerge herself in studying her
case files. She didn't want to think about anything other
than work. She wanted no thoughts of Frances, Mrs.
Cheryl or Sean, just work.

A Woman's Fury

CHERYL sat up in her bed and immediately covered her face in shame. She felt horrible now and had hoped it was all just a terrible dream until she felt Matthew's naked body lying in bed next to her. She turned her head slowly gazing upon him as he slept so peacefully. She couldn't remember the last time she felt truly peaceful. It surely wasn't recently, not since she had met him had she felt peaceful. He was ruining her life and now, he was in her bed.

Matthew now lay in the bed that she and her husband had slept in together for years until he had driven the wedge between them. They had always managed to put aside their differences and share the bed before, but now that Matthew had come along, the distance between them had driven Andrew into the guest room. Cheryl couldn't stop her tears now. She quickly got out of bed, rushed to the bathroom and took a shower. She knew she would never be able to cleanse the sin from her soul, but she scrubbed her body as if she were trying her best to do exactly that.

Matthew was waiting for her in bed when she returned. He smiled at her as she stood there eyeing him angrily and tightened her robe.

"Get out!" Cheryl said with anger in her voice.

"Why? Is he on his way here? What time is it?" Matthew asked. Cheryl's eyes grew smaller as her fury began to grow more intense.

"I said get out! Get out now, Matthew! I want you gone! Out of my bed and out of my life! Get out and keep going! Don't ever call me, or come back here again! Do you understand me! It is over! You are not who I want to be with. I love my husband and you have no place in my life! It's over!"

Matthew looked at her, smiling wickedly, then slowly got out of bed. Cheryl was angry, but turned her head as he approached her in the nude.

"Really baby? I'm sorry to hear that. I was looking forward to one more good time before hubby came home. No worries. I'll come back later..."

"No! Don't ever come back! Ever!" Cheryl snapped loudly.

Matthew raised an eyebrow. He tilted his head slightly as he stared at her. Then he scoffed.

"Did I upset you? Well, now, that is interesting. Tell me what you think you know about me, baby doll." Matthew said as he placed his hands on her hips. Cheryl immediately swung her hand at him and slapped him hard on his cheek.

Matthew stared at her for a moment, but suddenly smiled wickedly as she spoke.

"I said … Get Out! Now!" She practically growled in anger at Matthew.

"If I refuse to leave? Then what? You are much too beautiful for me to be afraid of, or intimidated by. Why don't we just kiss and make up. Never mind that you slapped me. I don't mind a little rough play, but uh…you know that already."

Cheryl pushed away from him and walked over to the telephone.

"Leave now, or I'm calling the police to have you escorted out!"

Matthew scoffed softly at her.

"Are you serious? Really Cheryl? The police?"

Matthew shook his head in disapproval, but continued to smile at her. He scoffed again as she lifted the receiver. Matthew's facial expression did not change, but he raised his hands as if trying to soothe her as he spoke.

"Okay baby. I don't want to make you angry. I'll go, for now anyway, but rest assured, we are not done, not by a long shot. This relationship ends when I say it ends and not before! You think you can just say no more and it's over? Think again baby! You'll keep putting out for as long as I want you to. I am the one in control here, not you and sure as hell not that idiot reverend that you married."

Matthew turned toward the bedroom door, but paused and added almost in admiration of Andrew.

"Although, I must admit that he has good taste in houses, cars and women. You know...the finer things in life. He's really kinda admirable so he can't be all idiot, just mostly. Of course, given the opportunity to have any of his possessions, I'd take you over any of the others even though you clearly hate me. I'd rather have you than anything else. You are just way too tempting especially when you say no to me. It drives me crazy, baby. I'll see you later, okay? Don't break my poor little heart this time."

Matthew smirked, blew a kiss at her, and then walked out of the room. He walked back to the living room where his clothes were still on the floor, put them back on and left silently. Cheryl watched from the window as he walked out of the house, waved at her happily, got into his car, and drove out of sight.

Cheryl didn't want to sleep in the bed anymore. She grabbed all the sheets and blankets and quickly tossed them over the side of the stairs. She wanted to just toss them out of the window, but she didn't want to get the neighbors attention, so she dragged them all out to the trash. Then she drove to a furniture store where she picked out a new bed and told them she wanted to have it delivered and installed immediately. Unfortunately, the earliest time they could do this was tomorrow, so she had to figure out something to tell Andrew. She couldn't really concentrate on what she should tell him because time was flying and she had to talk to Rachel.

A Prideful Fall

NOW IT was up to Cheryl to talk to Rachel and try
to convince her that she was not a bad person, but
simply human. She acted on her impulses rather than
thinking things over and it had cost her...everything. She
would lose her marriage, her reputation was soon to be
tarnished with an irremovable stain and she would,
most likely be put out of Andrew's home if he wanted
her to leave, but she had hoped he would find it in his
heart to forgive her. She didn't want to live without him.
She knew this, but she also knew that it would be hard
for them to pick up the pieces.

She hadn't thought about those things before when she
was angry at Andrew or during sex with Matthew, but
she couldn't stop thinking about them now. Her guilt
and shame grew and grew as she sat behind the steering
wheel of her car and wept silently. Somehow, she had to
find a way to be forgiven for her mistake.

Then, she thought about Matthew. He was so different
from Andrew. He was young, impulsive and exciting.

Andrew was never as spontaneous as Matthew. She thought about how she had easily surrendered her body to him this afternoon right there in her own house. She could not turn away from him on a sexual level. She didn't even fight him when he carried her to her bedroom. Matthew was the tiger in bed that her body craved and ached for desperately, but Andrew was the stability, protection and reliability that she wanted in her life.

"If only Andrew behaved more like Matthew...." She began, but shook her head quickly to remove that thought from her head. She closed her eyes and whispered a quick prayer.

"God, please help me get through this."

She spoke softly as she gripped her steering wheel tightly and wept for a few moments in the parking lot of the furniture store. Several people walked by, pretending not to notice her as she cried, but a few stared blatantly. Cheryl seemed oblivious to the passersby as she cried. Then when her tears began to subside, she wiped her eyes slowly as she looked at her reflection in the rearview mirror, eyeing herself carefully as she analyzed her appearance.

Cheryl had become just a shell of the proud woman she used to be. She was always much too proud to ask for help before she got married, then when she married Andrew she was proud of her husband. She was even proud of the encouraging growth of their church. Her pride had even allowed her to hook Matthew's attention, but she was definitely not a proud woman now.

She had become desperate. She was desperate for understanding, forgiveness, comfort and Andrew. Her pride had been her undoing. Her sin had made her realize this, but it was too late to change things now.

"What can I do? How can I go on without Andrew?" She thought to herself.

She started her car and headed for Rachel's apartment in spite of her continuous falling tears.

Sins of the Flesh,
Human and Alive,
The Eyes of God

RACHEL parked her car then headed toward her apartment building. She had almost reached the door, when she heard someone call her name. She hesitated, looking around cautiously for the source of the voice and spotted Cheryl rushing up to her. Rachel wanted to run inside of the building and lock the door securely behind her, but she remained frozen in terror instead. She tried to smile politely through her horrified expression.

"Oh, hello Mrs. Cheryl. I was just…" she began politely, but Cheryl cut her off.

"Let's save the pleasantries for the inside. I don't want to talk out here." Cheryl replied.

She spoke quickly as she looked around. Rachel stared at her as her fears began to arise again.

"She doesn't even want to be seen in public with me. This is worse than I thought." Rachel panicked inside as her thoughts continued.

"Cheryl Montgomery, The Saint, and Rachel Jensen, the whore she is trying to save." Rachel blinked as her thoughts continued to assault her brain viciously.

"She is taking a big chance coming here to talk to me. I should just confess everything so that she can help me. Who knows, maybe she can help me to become clean again."

Rachel made her way to the elevator of the apartment building followed closely by Cheryl who was also very quiet.

"Maybe that is why she has come! She has come because she knows I'm unclean and she has come to help me. Of course! I will confess everything to her! I will tell her the truth and be right with God again. Oh, thank you God! Thank you for sending her to me! What a relief!" Rachel began to smile again.

She felt better and believed that everything would be fine now. Cheryl was going to tell her how to free herself of this sinful nature for the last time. No more slip ups with Sean or anyone else. Cheryl would help her to be the Christian that she wanted to be and truly live her life for God.

"A true woman of God has come to stop me from condemning myself even further." She thought.

When they reached Rachel's apartment, she unlocked the door and allowed Cheryl to walk inside first.

"I'm sure it's not much compared to what you are used to, but it keeps me warm, dry and comfortable. God has blessed me tremendously, so I am very thankful for it. Please, make yourself comfortable Mrs. Cheryl." Rachel said as she closed the door behind her and put her keys on the table.

Rachel remembered visiting the Montgomery house when her parents died. She was grieving them and growing bitter with God, but instead she sought their help. They took her in immediately and prayed with her. She began to hold to God once more, but now, she felt that she was drifting away from him again. Cheryl had come to rescue her for a second time.

Cheryl walked into the apartment and sat down on the sofa. Her eyes scanned the apartment slowly. There were large windows, paintings that weren't too pricey, but very nice and everything was neat and clean. Rachel's apartment was lovely. Cheryl was used to luxurious spaces, but she didn't feel out of place inside of Rachel's apartment.

Cheryl looked at Rachel while she tried to relax on the soft cushioned sofa. The sofa was comfortable, but

Cheryl was uncomfortable. She didn't know exactly where to begin with Rachel, but she knew she had to begin.

"Rachel, I must confess that this is an unusual call but I must talk with you. I simply must. If I don't talk to you, I don't know what will happen." She began.

Rachel nodded in agreement, causing Cheryl to freeze immediately. "Oh my God! She knows!" Cheryl thought as a look of terror began to grow across her face.

Rachel began to pace around the apartment in order to avoid eye contact with Cheryl. She had to tell everything if she were going to be free of this mess. She took a deep breath and began to speak.

"Yes, I know. I'm glad you came to talk to me. I didn't think anyone knew, but I'm very glad that you found out. I would like the chance to explain why I did what I did though, if you will allow me just a moment to do so."

Rachel paced the room back and forth trying to put her words, feelings and thoughts together as Cheryl's look of terror became one of confusion. She stared at Rachel strangely and thought as she watched her pace nervously.

"What in the world is she talking about? Is this a kind of trap? What is going on?"

Cheryl continued to look at Rachel who slowly folded her hands together in front of herself as began to speak.

"Well, it all started when I went to that dreadful club. It's a night club called Optical Illusion. I went there for the first time for Frances' birthday party." She paused and looked at Cheryl who still looked confused. Cheryl spoke softly, shaking her head slightly.

"Rachel, a nightclub? What..." Cheryl began, but Rachel interrupted desperately trying to plead her case to Cheryl. Cheryl was confused.

"What did a nightclub have to do with what is happening between me and Andrew?" Cheryl wondered, but then decided to let Rachel continue with her story.

"I know I shouldn't have gone there, I do, but I couldn't say no to Frances. She was so disappointed..."

Rachel paced over to the large window and stood in silence. She couldn't stand to look at the reaction Cheryl was having to hearing her story. If she were going to confess, she would have to do it without looking at Cheryl and seeing the disappointment in her eyes. Rachel stared out the window of her apartment and continued to explain. Cheryl continued to listen in silence.

"She told me that her friends had put it together for her and they were having it there. I didn't plan to stay long, it's just that Frances....well, she can be very bossy sometimes, even bratty if she doesn't get her way. She began to have a fit, so I told her I would go. I don't know. I felt as if it might be good for me." Rachel remembered how she felt that night as she tried to put her feelings into words.

"I felt like, well, I was curious, but I...actually wanted to go. She didn't have to talk to me too long to convince me that I should go. A part of me wanted to go, but a part of me wanted to do what was right. I was confused, but gave in to my curious human nature. I wanted to see the club for myself, to experience it, to have fun, to be....normal."

Cheryl slowly lifted one hand and covered her mouth. This is not what she expected to hear from Rachel at all. Rachel had been so quiet in church. She was one member who Cheryl never would have thought of as wanting to go into a nightclub, but no one was absolutely perfect. Cheryl wanted to comfort Rachel immediately and tell her that she was normal, but she waited for her to finish her story.

Rachel felt the guilt of what she had done returning to her as she spoke, but she knew she had to confess everything or she would never be free of it. She took a deep breath, closed her eyes then continued.

"I know I really should not have gone there, but I felt like ...well, I felt ... honestly Mrs. Cheryl, I felt so alone. I felt

ugly and unloved. I wanted someone to love me....
physically, but I ...didn't plan on finding anyone there. I
had been feeling this way for quite some time. I know
God's love should be adequate and take those impure
thoughts away from us, but...My body wanted sex. It had
been years since I've done it Mrs. Cheryl. I don't know
why, but the urges came to me quite suddenly. Does that
make me a slut?"

Rachel turned away from the window and looked at
Cheryl who blinked hard as Rachel spoke. She was
feeling the exact same thing that Rachel had described,
so she knew what Rachel needed to hear. Cheryl rose
from the sofa, walked over to Rachel, held her hand and
shook her head as tears formed in her eyes. Her voice
trembled with emotion as she spoke to Rachel
attempting to soothe them both with her words.

"No Rachel. It makes you alive...human and alive. Not a
slut. You are not a slut at all. You are made of flesh and
our flesh craves excitement sometimes. If we didn't have
flesh, we wouldn't be alive. We'd be robots, cold and
unfeeling. That's not what God wants for us. He wants us
to have sensations, desires and experience pleasure.
They are emotions that all of God's perfect living
creations experience, so do not refer to yourself as a slut
again. You are HIS creation, nothing less. " Cheryl said
softly.

Rachel began to feel better, but her story was not over, so she continued.

"Thank you for the kind words Mrs. Cheryl, but I'm afraid there is more to the story."

Cheryl nodded and listened as Rachel took another deep breath and began again.

"I met a guy there named Sean. He worked there as a door attendant and was really nice to me in fact, he showed me where to find Frances, but I didn't make it to her because...We...well he.... He kissed me and I didn't stop him. He touched me...Mrs. Cheryl...I enjoyed it. Please don't think I'm a Harlot. I'm not, am I? I don't do these things, but this...it just...it just happened so quickly."

Rachel felt the tears beginning to flow from her eyes in spite of her attempts to stop them. She turned away from Cheryl, facing the window, but Cheryl took hold of her shoulders and turned her back. She looked into Rachel's eyes as she spoke.

"I'm not judging you Rachel. It's not my place to judge you. Believe me. I understand. I understand better than you think I do. I know you are hurting, thinking less of yourself and even doubting your own Christianity. I know all those things, but I also know that all those negative things are not of God."

Rachel felt tears in her eyes, but continued anyway. She had almost finished, so she forced herself to go on with the story in spite of the shame and anguish her heart felt.

"Frances didn't see me, but I heard her. She thinks I wanted to embarrass her in front of her friends, but I couldn't tell her that I was there letting him touch me like that. Then, I went back to the same club with my co-workers and saw him again. I didn't plan to…this time….I…let…We had sex. I felt so cheap. It happened in the employee's locker area at the club. I know I should have waited until I am married, but…. I felt so alone, Mrs. Cheryl. My body turned against me and now, I have sinned in the eyes of God." Rachel quickly pulled away from Cheryl, ran toward the sofa, fell to her knees and hid her face on the sofa cushion as she wept hard.

Perfect Creation

CHERYL walked over to the sofa and sat next to Rachel's head as it rested. She reached over and stroked her hair gently.

"There there now Rachel. Everyone makes mistakes. We are only human. God understands this. God created us to desire companionship. What you did was only natural. It's nothing to be ashamed of at all. You think God has turned his back on you because you had sex? What do you believe married couples do? They have sex. God does not condemn us for having sex."

Cheryl continued to stroke Rachel's hair soothingly as she took a breath, then continued to attempt to ease Rachel's conscience.

"Aside from that, God loves us and knows our flaws better than we do, yet he has not turned his back on us. We may feel that he has, but he is always there. It is times like these that he carries us, but we are so filled with emotions that we don't necessarily see that he is with us until much later. You think what you did is an unforgivable act against God, but you did no such thing. In spite of the guilt, shame and resentment that you feel, you must remember that God is loving, kind, merciful and just. He is able and willing to forgive anything we place before him. We need to remember this and to forgive ourselves as well."

Rachel looked at Cheryl and wiped her eyes slowly. Cheryl smiled and continued to speak to Rachel. Rachel began to believe Cheryl's words were truly from God.

"Believe me Rachel, God loves you even now that you think you have done something terribly wrong. In his eyes, you are still his perfect creation. His mercy is everlasting period so I think the real problem here is you. You cannot forgive yourself for what you have done, but God already has."

Rachel looked at Cheryl and attempted to calm her sobs. Cheryl had definitely put her mind at ease. Rachel began to breathe slow deep breaths to stop her crying fit. She looked at Cheryl who was crying silently herself now.

"Oh Mrs. Cheryl! Thank you! Thank God for you!" Rachel sobbed loudly.

Rachel flung her arms around Cheryl and wept again. Cheryl embraced Rachel tightly and cried as well. Rachel thought she was overwhelmed by hearing her problem, but she could not be further from the truth. Cheryl had been crying in response to her own problems. The guilt she felt had driven her to tears while she spoke to Rachel.

Hearing Rachel's confession simply made Cheryl think of her own disturbing dilemma. She wished her problem was as simple as Rachel's but that was not the case. Cheryl's problem involved a husband, a lover and immorality. Cheryl needed to tell someone about it and decided that Rachel was the perfect person to hear her own confession because God had chosen her to hear Rachel's guilt laden confession.

Cheryl knew she would have a hard time confessing her infidelity to Rachel, but like Rachel had stated she knew it was the right thing to do. She hoped it would help her to think clearly as well as help her to forgive herself for hurting Andrew and Matthew as well. Cheryl knew that she cared for Matthew, which was why she couldn't say no to him, but she loved her husband.

The two women comforted each other silently clinging to each other tightly as they poured their emotions into their streams of falling tears. They did not fight the onset of tears. They both believed it to be a healthy release of the frustrations they had been feeling over the past few days.

A little while later, Rachel was feeling better and began to play the part of a proper host to her visitor. She rose to her feet, wiped the last of her tears away and smiled politely at Cheryl, who also wiped her tears. Rachel laughed softly as she spoke.

"I'm so sorry Mrs. Cheryl. I didn't even offer you anything to drink or to eat. Would you like something? I've been a terrible host. This is your first visit to my place. I must apologize for my terrible manners." she stated politely.

She walked into the kitchen and began to search for something to drink. She was feeling dehydrated from crying so much. She quickly grabbed a bottle of water and brought one back for Cheryl.

Cheryl took the bottle water and drank. She hadn't realized how thirsty she was before now and was thankful for the cool water.

"Thank you Rachel. This makes up for all the mistakes you made earlier. I am feeling much better thanks to you." Cheryl smiled as she spoke to Rachel who smiled back.

Cheryl wanted to feel better about her life, but she was struggling with telling Rachel about it. Rachel was still wiping her eyes after crying so hard. She looked at Cheryl, who remained in silent thought. Rachel began to feel conscious of her appearance.

"I must look terrible. I better clean myself up." She thought to herself then she excused herself to Cheryl.

"Mrs. Cheryl, please excuse me, I need to clean up. I'm a bit of a mess. Please, feel free to help yourself to anything you like. I'll be right back." Rachel said as she headed to the bathroom.

Rachel turned on the water and began to wash her face. Then she stared at herself in the mirror. She didn't feel so disgusted with herself anymore and she was able to think more clearly now. She lowered her head and splashed her face again, then the thought occurred to her.

"Cheryl had no idea of what was bothering me yet she had stated that she wanted to talk. Cheryl …had something to say…. of her own and wanted to share it with me!" Rachel's eyes grew wide as she thought about it.

"Oh my God!" Rachel thought to herself. She quickly dried her face and exited the bathroom.

Cheryl had been debating on whether she should leave the apartment or not while Rachel was in the bathroom and decided on taking the coward's way out and leaving before actually confessing her sins to Rachel.

"I should leave. I don't want to talk about it now. She doesn't know anything about Andrew and me. She will think I'm a tramp and never trust me again if I tell her anything about what has happened. She may even feel that I am not qualified to tell her that God still loves her because I'm a sinner too. I'm even more of a sinner than she is come to think of it. All the joy she is feeling because she has confessed her sins will be lost if I confess to her now. I don't want to do that, so I'll just have to find another way to solve this problem."

Cheryl thought as she sat on the couch, then another thought occurred to her.

"So, this means, Andrew may not know yet either. I may not have to confess to him. I will just go home and stop ignoring him. I will treat him the way he deserves to be treated and he will never even find out about my infidelity with Matthew. He will think I was upset over my weight or something. Yes, I should definitely leave now."

She slowly rose to her feet and began to make her way toward the door when Rachel rushed back into the living room. Cheryl immediately stopped in her tracks and stood there silently with her back to Rachel, but she could feel the stare emanating from her eyes across the room. Cheryl didn't know what Rachel was thinking of her at that moment.

She could still leave if she didn't want to talk to Rachel. Cheryl knew that Rachel was not going to stop her from leaving if that was what she wanted to do so, but Cheryl began to wonder if she wanted to leave or not.

"I was almost gone. What do I tell her now?"

She thought, as she stood there still refusing to face Rachel, until she decided that she should at least face her in spite of her body's reluctance to turn. She tried to weigh the pros and cons of leaving versus staying as she prepared to talk to Rachel.

"If I stay, I'll confess everything, more than likely anyway, but if I leave, she won't know anything and I could keep my reputation safe. No one will know that I cheated on Andrew or say nasty things about me…. Except when Andrew files for a divorce, which he will do unless, I can think of a way to keep him."

The more she thought about it, the worse she began to feel. Staying was soon the only option for her. She needed to tell Rachel and believed that was why God led her here to Rachel's apartment. She had heard Rachel's reason for being so distant and ashamed so now, she knew it was her turn to share her own guilt-plagued emotions.

Purpose

CHERYL slowly lifted her head and turned to Rachel, who stared at her as if she too were struggling with finding the right words. Cheryl fought the tears as she looked away quickly. Rachel took advantage of the awkward moment now.

"I believe you want to say something Mrs. Cheryl. That is why you came here isn't it? God led you here to me so that you could talk to me about whatever is bothering you as well. I am more than willing to listen if you will tell me about it. I can even offer some sort of advice. It may not be as good as your own advice, but I'm willing to try and help in any way I possibly can." Rachel said as she approached her slowly.

Cheryl shook her head and looked downward as she spoke. She could not make eye contact with Rachel or she would break down and cry again. She was tired of crying. She tired of hiding, lying and cheating. She wanted to be free of the guilt, shame and relentless pain

Tyler

in her heart. She wanted to be in Andrew's arms and to know that he still loved her no matter what she had done. Andrew was not God, so receiving his forgiveness maybe impossible.

"I...Rachel, it's not important. I am glad you are feeling better."

 Cheryl was still reluctant to share. She knew it was the right thing to do, but she didn't want to feel that Rachel was passing judgment upon her. She wasn't feeling so brave about revealing her own imperfections and indiscretions.

Rachel continued her attempt at coaxing Cheryl into talking to her.

"You said you wanted to talk to me and that you wouldn't take no for an answer, but I am the one who did all the talking, and confessing so far."

She approached Cheryl cautiously as if she were trying to snare a butterfly that she didn't want to take flight before she could catch it. She continued to speak soothingly as she stepped even closer to Cheryl who was still struggling with her thoughts.

Cheryl continued to shake her head. She wanted to think clearly, but all she could think of was how Rachel would not respect her any longer if she knew the truth. Her fears began to cloud her reasoning and she covered her eyes as Rachel moved closer to her attempting to soothe her.

"You have something to talk about Mrs. Cheryl. Please, don't hold it in. You know that is no good for you. You saw how my guilt controlled me. It was very stressful and that's not healthy at all. I couldn't think clearly, I couldn't sleep, I could barely eat … it is horrible to think that everyone that you care about will think less of you because you are only human. Why don't you share your problem with me? I can help, well, maybe, but it's worth a try."

Cheryl felt as if her heart dropped into her stomach, aching terribly all the way down. The guilt of her deception began to eat away at her brave exterior. She sat down and hid her face attempting to shield her shame. She couldn't speak now that she was crying so hard. Her chest heaved from the convulsions brought on by her now painful cries. Cheryl believed that her sin was truly unforgiveable and she knew that nothing on Earth could save her from losing the only man she ever truly loved now.

Rachel had no idea of what was bothering Cheryl, but she really wanted to help her feel better about it. She rushed over to her side and hugged her tightly while she sobbed relentlessly. Rachel comforted Cheryl just as Cheryl had comforted her earlier.

Cheryl felt like she had no one to turn to. The women at the senior home would never understand her problem. They would raise their eyebrows and stare at her strangely when she tried to get them to talk about sex, except Ms. Stewart. She was the only one who would talk freely about sex while the other women shook their heads disapprovingly. Even the passersby made strange faces when Ms. Stewart would respond to Cheryl's sex related questions.

Cheryl knew how Rachel felt about sex. She knew Rachel felt uneasy talking about it, just like most of the other Christians did, but Cheryl also knew that Rachel needed to overcome this if she were really going to help her with her problem. She didn't want her to be so shy with talking about sex any longer.

Cheryl knew she had to teach Rachel that sex was a part of life, a gift from God and nothing to be ashamed of talking about.

"Rachel, I need to be honest with you if you want to hear my story, so I need to ask you something."

"I want to help in any way that I can Mrs…" Rachel began, but Cheryl cut her off.

"Please, stop with the formalities. Just call me Cheryl. I am a woman, just like you. I'm not your aunt, grandmother or any other relative. Just Cheryl, okay?"

Rachel raised her eyebrows instinctively. She was obviously surprised to hear Cheryl speaking like that, but nodded and accepted what she just said. She could tell that Cheryl was frustrated already and did not want to aggravate her any more than necessary.

"Okay, Cheryl. What would you like to know?"

"Are you uncomfortable talking about sex? My problem concerns sex and if I'm going to open up and share with you, there are things I need to discuss that are pretty explicit. I don't want you to feel uncomfortable at all. I need to know that you can handle the discussion before I begin."

Cheryl watched Rachel carefully who clearly grew uncomfortable just as Cheryl thought she would. Cheryl sighed and shook her head slightly but began to speak.

"Rachel, sex is not a bad thing. Sex is the union of two people who care deeply for each other most of the time anyway. How can it be ugly if it is involved in the creation of one of God's most precious gifts? You think it's ugly, don't you?"

Cheryl waited silently watching Rachel who looked away from Cheryl for a moment, but then spoke.

"I think it is ugly when you aren't married and get so caught up in lust that you allow some guy to have you in a locker room. If you are married, yes, I believe it is a beautiful thing."

Cheryl shook her head and scoffed.

"You've clearly never been married, Rachel. When you get married, you will find that there are things you have to give up to keep your husband happy. When you do, you will remember what I've told you. Sex is definitely beautiful most of the time. It's God's way of creating life through us and all things of God are beautiful, therefore sex is beautiful. I don't believe that he meant for us to look at sex as another task to perform. I think he meant us to enjoy it, to receive and to give each other physical pleasure from it. We are very physical creations you know."

Cheryl looked at Rachel who sat silently. She wanted Rachel to say something, but that didn't happen because Rachel had never heard Cheryl talk like this before and honestly didn't know what to say. Then Rachel finally thought of what she wanted to say in response to Cheryl's statement.

"Cheryl, I believe I have to agree with you. Sex is beautiful. When I was with Sean, I didn't feel dirty during sex. It was afterward that I started to feel, well, less than a woman. I started thinking about what everyone would say about me if they knew and that worried me. I thought they would think that Christians don't do this kind of thing and just pronounce me another sleazy sinner Jezebel. That wasn't a nice thought. Sean was very nice to me and he was a gentle lover, but I wasn't comfortable with it because I kept wondering about what people would say if they knew…that I actually liked it. I didn't think I was supposed to like having sex, but I was surprised, embarrassed and ashamed that I did."

Rachel had not realized what she was saying. She had just shared even more with Cheryl, but it wasn't what she had intended to do. She was no longer ashamed of herself.

"Christians tend to clam up when it comes to sex, Rachel. No one wants to talk about it even though it is an important part of life. Most of us do look at it as a curse that is upon us from Adam and Eve's sin but we cannot ignore our needs and desires for it because it is how God designed us. I'm not saying we should just jump into bed with anyone, but we shouldn't feel bad after having sex with someone we care about because that is what God wants for us. He wants us to enjoy companionship."

Cheryl took a deep breath to further compose herself as Rachel slowly nodded in agreement.

"I believe that is a good point Cheryl. I think that sex is a hard subject for a lot of people to discuss, but especially hard for Christians, which probably make us need to discuss this issue even more than those who are not Christians. I never even thought about that before."

Rachel's mind began to absorb the words she had spoken. She began to understand Cheryl even better.

"That is right, Rachel. We need to remember that God did not tell us not to do it or talk about it. Everyone has their own views, opinions, and the such regarding sex, but how else will we get answers to questions if we don't ask or compare notes and findings with others about it? If we keep it bottled up inside and hide in shame when we do have sex, we aren't solving any problems. We are creating more of them because eventually, those feelings we have tried so hard to hide, just so that people won't think badly of us, will control our very lives."

Cheryl shook her head in disgust and blinked hard. Rachel understood what she was saying.

"They could also tear us away from God if we let them get to be that big. It is important for us to have an understanding congregation and reverend to help us deal with the issue of sex. We should remember that God puts people in our lives for this purpose. When we need support, guidance and help, he provides us with everyone that we need to help us through. We are not cursed by talking about our emotions, feelings or physical needs. You are right, we are very physical creations, but designed by God nevertheless."

Put God First

RACHEL looked at Cheryl and noticed that she had stopped crying. She nodded and gently squeezed Cheryl's hand.

"You are right, Cheryl. I agree with you." She added smiling approvingly.

Cheryl began to feel better about talking to Rachel and moved the conversation forward.

"I don't believe that oral sex is wrong either. I think that if it pleases your partner, then you should do it and they should not have to ask for it. That is the way I've felt for years. Andrew however, he thinks it's dirty and ungodly. We argue about it all the time."

Rachel hadn't thought about oral sex. She simply shook her head silently as Cheryl continued. She also wondered why Andrew thought it was wrong when

Cheryl thought it was not. She began to look at Cheryl questioningly.

"Well...." Rachel began to speak slowly, but Cheryl cut her off. She was determined to get her point across.

"I'm not ashamed of how I feel, or the fact that I don't mind giving my husband pleasure orally. I don't think it makes me any less of a Christian than anyone else. I'm sure I'm not the only one who thinks this way, but I don't know who else feels this way because no one is willing to talk about sex. It gets frustrating sometimes. It bothers me that the only woman I could talk to about sex was one of the little old ladies who lives in a senior home. This one in particular was open and honest about sex. She didn't clam up, but the others did, until she told them they were being silly. Then they all relaxed a little....very little and we had an interesting discussion. They didn't think Christians were comfortable with talking about sex so honestly either. We are automatically labeled because of our belief in God. It's almost as if we *aren't* supposed to feel anything, but we do. God made us just the same as he made everyone else. We are all human beings."

Rachel hadn't thought about that, but immediately agreed.

"You are right, Cheryl. When I've told people in the past that I am a Christian, they definitely change their demeanor. They grow silent and seem to be concentrating hard on what they say next. God forbid if they talk about sex or try to tell a sex related joke. They always stumble on it when I'm around."

Rachel began to laugh as she thought back.

"They act as if I have the power to condemn them for telling bad jokes." She couldn't contain her laughter now. She giggled loudly as Cheryl smiled.

"They do tend to get silly over things." Cheryl laughed too.

"Right? They think I have the power to strike them down with lightning or something if they use a curse word in front of me. It's funny. Of course I always pray for them, but it's funny at that moment."

"Well, we know that God gives us power over our enemies, but most people are not the enemy so they are quite safe. I know that they don't know this because if they did, they would relax. People just need an excuse though. They just need an excuse, any old excuse, to be utterly ridiculous and call us fanatics because of our belief in God. They don't think we are normal because we put God first while they put themselves first."

Cheryl began to look down again now after speaking those words. She knew that she had done exactly that and because she had, she was now looking at a possible divorce from her loving husband. She had been very selfish and unthinking. She shamed herself in her wrongful pursuit of sexual pleasure with another man. She knew it was wrong, but she was only being a woman in need of pleasure and not thinking about how it would affect anyone other than her at that moment. She didn't expect Matthew to be so adamant about seeing her and she didn't expect to reject her husband the way she instinctively had because of Matthew. Her lustful experiences with Matthew were ruining her life.

"Lately, I've been putting myself first and not God. I've been so selfish, angry and bitter, but I'm not sure exactly why. Andrew has always been so kind, patient and loving, but I believe that I have lost him forever now. I've treated him so badly that I don't even know where to begin. Bear with me Rachel. I've got to find the words for what I am feeling."

Cheryl leaned her back against the sofa and massaged her temples, closing her eyes as the tears began to form again. She wanted to maintain her composure long enough to share the story with Rachel, but knew she would be unable to.

Rachel noticed that Cheryl was struggling mentally and gently took hold of her hand to offer her some much needed support.

"It's okay, Cheryl. Take your time. I've got nothing to do tonight except to listen to you. I want to help and if it's God's will I shall."

Cheryl looked at Rachel as she smiled at her. She clutched Rachel's hand tightly with both of hers.

"Thank you Rachel. I will try to explain exactly what is going on. I believe that God led me to you for a reason. Perhaps, you are the one who will help me to get through this mistake and move on with my life."

Cheryl didn't hide her tears as they trickled from her eyes. Rachel nodded slowly in silence as Cheryl slowly began her story.

"Andrew and I met when we were in school. It was a long time ago. Well, we didn't get married right away because I wasn't sure about it. I wanted to make sure that when I did get married, it would last forever. Andrew wanted to get married right after we graduated, but I didn't. He asked me when we were close to graduating, but I said no. He believed that I didn't love him like he loved me, so we drifted apart for a while. I honestly thought I would never see him again, so naturally, I dated other guys."

"I wish I could tell you that nothing happened with some of them, but that is not the case. I dated them and even had sex with a couple, but I knew that nothing serious could come from the relationships."

"Then one day out of the blue, I saw him. He immediately remembered me and we began to date again. He told me that he was a Christian and that he was studying to be a reverend. I was happy for him of course, then he invited me to attend a church service with him. I felt compelled to become a Christian as well. So I did. Soon afterward, we were married. I'm not sorry I married Andrew. I was young and in love, but he was very special to me. He still is and as far as I am concerned, he always will be."

Cheryl took a breath then continued. Rachel held her hand but remained silent. She did not want to interrupt Cheryl's story.

"Andrew wanted to have children, but I found out from my doctor that I could not. I had an abortion previously and my body was never able to support another fertilized egg following it. Andrew had really wanted children, but he stayed with me anyway. I knew the news of my infertility broke his heart, but he put on a brave face and loved me nevertheless."

Cheryl's tears began to trickle down her cheeks. She lowered her head and shut her eyes tightly, but managed to continue speaking.

"He was always so good to me. He is a wonderful man. He's very considerate and generous. He always bought flowers for me, gifts and took me on expensive vacations. He gave me everything I wanted in life, in fact, he spoiled me rotten, but of course, I wanted more. I was never truly satisfied with what I had. I didn't see that God had blessed me when he gave me Andrew."

Cheryl took her free hand and wiped her tears away as she continued speaking. Rachel began to rub her shoulder.

"It's okay Cheryl. Take your time, breathe deeply. It will help you." Rachel said soothingly. Cheryl nodded silently, then went on with her story after taking a deep breath.

"Andrew would not give me oral sex. He thought it was unholy and sinful, so he would not do it for me. I showed him that it wasn't anything wrong with it and he continued to say it was wrong. I thought if I continued to do it for him, he would eventually do the same for me, but he stopped me from doing it for him. He kept saying it was dirty and we should not do that sort of thing. Whenever I did do it for him, he felt guilty and immediately after sex, he got on his knees and prayed."

Rachel continued to listen to Cheryl's story in silence. She had never thought of Andrew as a real man before. She wasn't sure what to think now. Cheryl continued to speak.

"The last time I did it for him, he told me that we both should pray and ask God to forgive us for doing such a vile thing with our bodies. I did just to calm him down, but I didn't believe it was wrong for me to do it. In my heart I believed it was fine, but Andrew was paranoid and asked me not to do that again. So the next time we were about to have sex, he jumped away from me when

I tried to do it for him. He told me not to do that to him. He didn't want it and it was unholy. I felt so stupid and ugly. I don't think he meant to make me feel that way, but it is how I felt."

Rachel hadn't done that with Sean either. She didn't have oral sex with anyone really. Not even Justin, but she didn't want to mention that to Cheryl because she didn't want her to feel bad about it. She knew that Cheryl was in an emotional state right now, so she wanted her to know that she was trying to comfort her and not judge her. Cheryl continued to share her story after taking a few moments to recover from what she just shared with Rachel. She was clearly fighting to suppress her swelling emotions.

"Well, I was frustrated with the whole thing and stopped trying to convince him. Of course, I was sexually frustrated because things had gotten so bad that Andrew was afraid to let me touch him. Then one day, I decided to go shopping for some lingerie. I hoped it might spice things up and get Andrew to change his mind about sex, but while I was shopping a young man approached me. He told me that he thought the outfit I was holding would look good on me and he'd love to see me wear it. I ignored him of course, but he kept complimenting me and he even held up some outfits saying this would look good on me too. I was completely embarrassed and walked out of the store, but he followed me. He was very persistent. He offered to buy me lunch, but I said no. I left and went home."

Rachel's eyes grew wide as Cheryl took another breath then hesitated. She looked at Rachel, who quickly blinked her eyes and returned her face to normal.

"I'm listening, Cheryl, please continue." Rachel said. Cheryl smiled slightly.

"What? Did you think I was a robot or something? I'm human too." Cheryl said teasingly. Rachel smiled in reply as Cheryl continued with her story.

"Then, the next day, I thought I would try again, but the same young man came back. He immediately started following me around the store again. So, I left, but this time, he ran up to me and handed me a bag from the store. He bought me an outfit and said he still wanted to see me wear it. I was flattered, but there was no way I was going to comply with him. I dropped the bag and left. I didn't go back there for a few days, then Andrew and I had a huge fight. I felt frustrated, confused and even repulsive. I felt like he didn't care enough about me to even try to please me sexually. I was lost and confused and in my depressed state, I remembered the young man who had pursued me. I thought if Andrew did not want me, I would find someone who would. I went back to the store and began to look at the things. Just when I thought he would not come back, he did. He spotted me and was more cautious when he approached me this time. I had done all but scream rape before, but this time, I giggled and flirted back with him. I began to feel beautiful again. Then he suggested that we go to a hotel. I could have said no, but I said yes."

The Pact: The Hands of the Lord

RACHEL'S eyes grew wide as she held in her gasp. She was obviously surprised to hear Cheryl's confession. Cheryl knew she would be and did not panic at all. She continued to speak in spite of Rachel's obvious shock at the revelation.

"That's right. I went to this hotel room with this young man and we had sex there for the first time. He did all the things that Andrew would not and I enjoyed being with him, but afterward, I felt dirty. I was cheating on my husband and it made me feel sick to my stomach when I thought about it. Yes, Matthew did please me. He enjoyed pleasing me unlike Andrew, but Andrew was the man I loved, the man I married and the man I wanted to spend the rest of my life with. I knew this even as I was lying there with Matthew. He could never be what Andrew was to me."

Cheryl took another deep breath as the tears fell from her eyes. She covered them briefly, breathing hard as she did. Then she removed her hand from her face and looked at Rachel who covered her own mouth in surprise, and sadness.

Cheryl could not speak for a moment as she fought against her approaching crying fit. She breathed hard again, closing her eyes then wiping the tears from her face. She looked down at her lap to keep herself from looking at Rachel. She felt too ashamed for words now.

Rachel slowly reached forward and took hold of Cheryl's hand squeezing it tightly.

"Cheryl, it's okay. I'm not judging you. It's not my place. Not at all. I only want to help you to make it right." Rachel said.

Cheryl gasped hard as she fought for composure. She felt her chest swelling with emotion and took another deep breath to ease the pressure.

"Matthew and I met almost every day for nearly a month. He knew I was married because I told him that was why I could not spend the night with him. He didn't say anything at first, but later on, he started being very jealous. He wanted me to spend more time with him and began to threaten to tell Andrew if I didn't come and see him. He called our house while we were at church

Sunday and Andrew heard the message he left for me. Andrew asked me who he was..."

Cheryl couldn't take it any longer. She began to cry as she spoke to Rachel now.

"I had no choice but to lie. I lied to my husband! I just couldn't tell him that I had been sleeping with Matthew while he was working hard making money to support me. I feel so ashamed. I betrayed him and lied to him about it. What kind of a woman would do that to her husband? Andrew hasn't done anything wrong. He stuck by me when we found out that I couldn't have children even though he was disappointed. He could have went out and got someone else pregnant, but he didn't. He stayed with me and comforted me when I should have comforted him. He is a good God fearing man who loves me unconditionally, but I betrayed him because he wouldn't perform oral sex on me."

Cheryl closed her eyes tightly crying loudly as Rachel embraced her.

"It was stupid and selfish. Selfish and stupid, but I can't take it back now. What am I going to do now? I can't live without Andrew, but Matthew keeps calling. He will tell Andrew everything unless I tell him first. Andrew will most likely leave me and file for a divorce. I will be all alone, Rachel. I won't have Andrew anymore!" Cheryl cried hard as Rachel continued her attempts to soothe her.

Rachel knew how Cheryl felt. She had wanted to be more of a comfort to her, but she didn't know exactly what she should say to her. She didn't want to tell her that it was wrong for her to cheat on her husband because Cheryl already knew that. She didn't want to say that it was foolish of her because she knew that as well. Rachel could not think of anything to say to Cheryl at all. She decided that the best thing to do was to be silent and continue to embrace her, allowing her to vent physically so that Cheryl could think more clearly afterwards, just as she had done for her.

"I don't know how to tell Andrew about it. I know I should tell him, but I don't even know where to begin. He is such a kind man. Rachel, this will break his heart. I never meant to hurt him. I just wanted my own pleasure. I put his needs aside and put my own first. I totally ignored him....and God! I turned away from them both because of my fleshly needs and desires. It was wrong I know, but I can't change it. God forgive me for what I've done. I just hope this doesn't destroy my marriage, but I honestly don't see any good coming from this."

Cheryl was inconsolable. She continued to weep as Rachel gently caressed her back.

"God will work it all out for you Cheryl. You will be amazed at what he can do, but you already know that he does great things. He can deliver you from this situation and prevent Andrew's heart from being hardened by this. If it is his will, your marriage will not be harmed, if the worst does happen, you will learn to go on with God's help. Don't cry. God has it all worked out for you. Just relax and trust him to handle it all. He will tell you what you should do."

Rachel didn't know what she was saying. She simply wanted to comfort Cheryl, but the words seemed to flow from her mouth effortlessly. She hadn't even planned on speaking to Cheryl, but when she wanted to ask her not to cry, the other words were spoken instead.

After crying for a while, Cheryl was sick with worry and it was getting late now, so Rachel invited her to stay the night.

"I should get back to Andrew. He will think the worst." Cheryl sounded like an exhausted helpless child. Rachel felt bad for her and was determined that she stay. She didn't want Cheryl to drive in this condition.

"Don't worry, Cheryl. I will call him and explain that you are here." She said.

Cheryl was exhausted and her body ached all over from her continuous crying. She felt stupid sitting there crying in front of Rachel like she had, but she began to feel better now because she had someone to talk to about the situation.

Rachel gave Cheryl a clean nightgown and showed her around the apartment. Cheryl began to relax and enjoy Rachel's company. Rachel in turn did the same. It was nice to have someone there to talk to and who didn't try to pass judgment on her for being a Christian. She had someone to talk to who understood that she was not perfect, but merely human. Both women were thankful for each other. They both had changed into their bedclothes and were watching a movie in the living room while eating popcorn, when Rachel came up with an idea.

"Cheryl, why don't we make a pact? We promise each other that when we have something we really need to talk about, we call each other. I cannot tell you how much better I feel now that I have shared my secret with you. I feel like I can handle things a lot better now rather than having the feeling that all eyes are on me and people are saying bad things about me. It is such a relief."

Rachel sighed deeply as if she were breathing for the first time today. She smiled at Cheryl who nodded silently.

"That is a good idea Rachel. I'm glad I could help you. I don't mind talking to you about your problems. I have been through the problems of a single woman, so, I understand them. The marriage problems, I'm not so good at, but of course, therein lies the dilemma.

Everything in life has to be learned and what better teacher in life than experience? I will learn as I go along, just as you will. God will make a way for both of us. We just have to be patient and accept his gracious gifts."

Cheryl blinked hard as she thought about Andrew again. She missed him, but she felt that staying the night at Rachel's place was the right thing to do.

Cheryl felt extremely tired now and wanted to sleep so Rachel showed her to the bedroom.

"Good night Cheryl. Sweet dreams and don't forget that God loves you!" Rachel said as she slowly closed the door.

"Thank you Rachel. I pray that you remember those words also. We both needed to be reminded of them today. Thank you again for reminding me. Good night, Rachel."

Cheryl eased into bed beneath the covers. She longed for Andrew and closed her eyes again as she thought of him. She wondered what he was doing now. She wondered if he even missed her or knew about her affair with Matthew.

"Knowing Matthew, he probably left a message telling Andrew everything. There is just no avoiding it now. Andrew will never forgive me for my betrayal, selfishness and stupidity. " Cheryl thought as she lay there and closed her eyes.

She knew she would not get much sleep that night and lay in bed slowly opening her eyes staring at the ceiling deep in thought as the tears began to trickle down the sides of her face stopping upon impact with the spongy pillow beneath her head. She wished she could explain why she had been so selfish, but she could not justify her actions now. She had turned her back on God and the love of her life because she thought she was right. The possibility of her being wrong had not occurred to her until now.

Cheryl lay awake in bed most of the night, weeping silently, contemplating any possible way of saving her marriage and praying for forgiveness.

Rachel on the other hand had felt better. She didn't feel like everyone believed that she was a slut because of Sean. She was practically at ease until she thought about Cheryl.

Rachel knew Cheryl was still in a great deal of agony and felt so helpless. She wanted to comfort Cheryl, but felt like she was unable to do this. She hated seeing Cheryl suffer as she was, but she also knew that God had a plan for her. She too had to be patient and allow God to reveal this plan to both of them.

"It's all in your hands, Lord." Rachel said as she lay beneath the covers on the sofa.

"It's always been in your hands. That will never change. Let your will be done and grant us the wisdom to see and accept what you have chosen for us instead of rejecting your plan and going our own way. Please forgive us for submitting to our sinful nature." Rachel added before dozing off.

Turning the Other Cheek

ANDREW had decided to work late that night so that when he got home, Cheryl would already be asleep. He drove along the path leading to the house deep in thought. He began to remember the argument that he and his wife had.

"Is sex all you expect from a marriage? A good marriage is more than just sex, Cheryl. There are other things ...." He had said to her, but she cut him off.

"Oh no you don't! I know there is more to marriage than just sex, but we both know that sex is an important part of it! You are trying to make me feel like some kind of tramp because I am asking you, my husband, to make me happy sexually."

Cheryl's eyes began to fill with tears as Andrew reached for her, but she quickly pulled away.

"Cheryl, come here. It's not that...don't...."

Cheryl was not going to submit to him so easily. She had always been a strong woman who was used to having things her way so she had to tell Andrew her thoughts. Andrew had fell in love with her because of her incredible strength. She had motivated him in many ways and he loved her truly for it. She was more than just a wife. She was his soul mate. He knew he would not have a life without her.

"No! Andrew, it's not that easy."

She said as she moved out of his reach. He watched her but did not pursue her. He knew she had something to say and would not relax until she had said it. He watched her move further away from him wiping her eyes slowly with the back of her hand.

"Cheryl..."

He watched her as she struggled for composure feeling helpless inside. He wanted to comfort his wife, but she interrupted his words with her own.

"I have always believed that you blamed me for my infertility and didn't think sex with me was worth the effort since I can't have children, but this makes it seem even more so. You aren't being honest with me Andrew, but I am being honest with you! You don't think I'm worth pleasing because I can't give you what you really want from me. I can't give you children."

Andrew stared at her as she spoke those words. He hadn't thought about her like that, yet she had apparently thought about this for a long time. He didn't see how she could have felt that way at all. He thought he had been good to her when they found out about her inability to have children, at least he had tried to be good to her. Hearing this accusation took him completely off guard.

"What? What are you talking about? I don't blame you for that. It is something that neither of us have any control over. You and I both know THAT is in God's hands not either of ours, so you tell me, Cheryl, how can I blame you for something that is beyond you? That just doesn't make sense! But you obviously spent a lot of time concentrating on that and convincing yourself to believe it."

Cheryl looked at him silently as tears fell down her cheeks. She blinked rapidly, attempting to stop them from flowing as Andrew moved closer to her and spoke. He shook his head and scoffed softly

"Cheryl, I don't know how you come up with these crazy things sometimes. That one was a real stretch, but wow! You twisted that to your benefit rather well. I should be so lucky to have you for a wife. You can argue about anything. You are really something else."

Andrew was attempting to lighten the mood and end the arguing as he slowly made his way closer to her. He wanted to take away her pain and knew that if she was blaming herself for the infertility she suffered from, he had to find a way to soothe her quickly.

"You know I love you more than anything on this planet, Cheryl. Please, don't blame yourself for things that you have no control over. Do you think I like seeing you torment yourself? Absolutely not. I thought I should answer that question before you because you might say yes, but I truly don't take pleasure in knowing you are in pain. You are my joy Cheryl, my wife, my absolute everything here on Earth."

Cheryl slowly calmed down as he gently caressed her arm, then shoulder. He moved closer to her and wrapped his arms around her waist.

"You know, sex is an important part of marriage. What do you say we try it now?" Andrew kissed her deeply and they made love that night.

Andrew enjoyed having sex with Cheryl. She was a very beautiful and desirable woman. She was the most desirable woman he had ever met and that did not change after they were married. He had been with other girls, but he always remembered being with Cheryl because she was hard for him to forget. She was the one he wanted to have in his life forever. He knew this when they were in school, but when she turned his marriage proposal down, he began to think that she didn't find him worthy as he found her. So, he dated other girls and began to fall into a depression because he knew he wanted her. Then he went to church with his parents one day and he found God.

 After that, he didn't have time to date other girls because he knew he wanted to be a minister. He wanted to give his life to The Lord completely. That was when God returned his Cheryl to him and this time, they were married. Andrew was happy with Cheryl and immediately began to spoil her. He didn't want her to have to struggle or beg anyone for anything as long as he had breath in his body. He wanted her to be well taken care of. It meant spending time away from her, but when he came home, it was always well worth it. He spoiled her, but she took good care of him as well. He was very happy with his loving wife.

Andrew splurged his money on her but also made it a point never to get so upset with her that he felt he had to shout at her. His parents were very much in love and never displayed such anger toward one another. Cheryl displayed her anger and yelled sometimes, but Andrew never reached this level. He believed that yelling was only one-step away from physical abuse, which he did not believe in.

Andrew shook his head in frustration as he parked the truck on the side of the house. He was still shocked from hearing Cheryl's accusing words during the argument. He didn't think she was the blame for not being able to have children. He had told her that before, but she was the one who insisted upon blaming herself. He tried to soothe her as best as he could but she fought against him, just as she usually did. He loved her ability and passion for speaking her mind, sometimes.

Andrew shifted the truck into the park gear and turned off the engine. He sat there in his truck thinking about his life with Cheryl. He felt that he drove her away from him with his constant refusal to make her happy sexually. He had blamed himself and now believed that she was going to leave him because she was no longer happy with him.

He knew Cheryl was right. Sex was an important part of marriage, but not the only important part. If two people don't please each other sexually, the marriage can and will suffer as he now found out the hard way. He began to wish he hadn't argued about it with her now. He wanted to tell her that he was sorry for making her so miserable and he wanted desperately to please her but he thought it was too late.

 He had done everything he could to keep her happy, except the one thing she wanted from him sexually. He had loved Cheryl for years even before they were married. She was his second love in his lifetime. God, of course, was his first. He had not intended to hurt her or push her away, but he could not turn away from God for her either. Despite his body's protests, he knew he could not turn away from God not even for her.

"What should I do, oh Lord?"

He closed his eyes and contemplated placing his head against the steering wheel. While he thought about possible answers, he began to grow exhausted and soon fell asleep.

Andrew had lost track of the time, but immediately snapped out of his uncomfortable slumber by the headlights of an approaching vehicle.

"Cheryl must have went looking for me."

He thought as he got out of the truck and walked around toward the front door.

He began to feel like things weren't so hopeless anymore. If she actually decided to go and look for him, he knew she missed him and wanted to work things out with him. He felt his heart jumping for joy inside his chest and rushed around the corner leading to the front door, but when he turned the corner, his smile quickly became a curious stare.

A young man stood there in front of the door, ringing the doorbell impatiently. He was so focused on the door, that he did not notice Andrew approaching. Andrew moved close enough for the young man to hear him, who quickly turned around as he spoke.

"May I help you?"

"What the…" The young man answered but stopped abruptly.

He looked at Andrew just as curiously as Andrew had looked at him. Andrew recognized the uniform from the restaurant and thought he may be a delivery person.

"You…look familiar. Oh, you were at the restaurant last night, right?" The young man said slowly. He squinted his eyes as he looked at Andrew.

"Yes, but I don't recognize you at all. Are you lost or something?" Andrew said.

"I'm not lost. I've been here before in fact, I've been here a few times before. I was looking for Cheryl. I need to talk to her. Is she around?" The young man said. He practically smirked as he spoke to Andrew, who began to grow angry.

Andrew's worst fears were now confirmed with the appearance of this boy. He wanted to remain calm in case things weren't as bad as he thought they were, but something told him that he was right to be angry with this man's appearance. He wouldn't have come this late at night to make a food delivery. Cheryl was having an affair with this boy. Andrew still did not want to believe it, but all the evidence pointed toward her infidelity.

"This! This is the one who she is seeing?" Andrew thought.

"So, YOU are Matthew!" Andrew clinched his fists as he spoke.

Matthew grinned proudly as Andrew frowned hard.

"Very good, Reverend! Yeah, I'm Matthew in the flesh! It's nice to finally meet... the man... who uh.... couldn't keep MY sweet treat happy. I'm not impressed with you either. I can definitely see why she was more interested in me." He turned toward Andrew practically laughing, but extending his hand as if he wanted to shake it in mocking admiration.

Andrew could feel his blood beginning to boil. His anger was just about at its limit. He felt his muscles in his face twitching as if he were fighting of a frown and failing miserably. He fought against the urge of rushing Matthew and punching him hard enough to lay him out cold right on the stairs. He attempted to shield his anger as he spoke to Matthew.

"Why did you come here? Did you come here to gloat? Did you come here to have sex with my wife in MY house! You have a lot of gall junior!"

Andrew was very angry now and the fact that Matthew couldn't stop smiling at his obvious anger made him want to choke the life from his body even at the risk of condemning his mortal soul.

"Ahh! Now that was a nice shot, rev. She told me it was okay to come. I don't know if that was your bed, but she said this house is hers. By the way, Cheryl doesn't call me junior. She thinks I'm man enough, even more of a man than you apparently especially when she's giving me...."

Andrew's blood was boiling now. The thought of this boy and his wife having sex in the same bed that he and Cheryl had slept in made him scowl. Andrew was enraged and raised his voice for the first time in as long as he could remember interrupting Matthew's words next degrading words abruptly.

"Get off my property! If you come back here, I'll have the police escort you off after I've snapped your worthless neck! Do you hear me boy! Don't bring your trashy mouth here again! Ever! Do you understand me?!"

Matthew's facial expression was one of fake surprise. He almost gasped...in mockery of Andrew.

"Oh! Is that what you call it? Trashy mouth? Oh, alright, reverend goody, but just to let you know nowadays we call it eating pussy, but the scientific name is cunnilingus. Now, don't quote me on that, but I think that's what it's called... but me...I'm a relatively simple man. I just call it ... "good", but with Cheryl...I call it...

"Heaven between legs." Mmmmm. Heaven...that's something you can relate to, right rev?" Matthew looked at Andrew's face as he spoke and his smile began to grow even wider.

Andrew's eyes were filled with anger and he gritted his teeth. Matthew knew he had gotten to Andrew and began to laugh heartily. He literally had a laughing fit as Andrew's rage grew more intense.

Andrew had heard all he could stand from Matthew and began approaching him rapidly in murderous rage. He wanted to choke Matthew, squeezing the life from his body until he had breathed his last annoying breath. If he could just get his hands on him, he knew that he would and no power on Earth would stop him from killing Matthew.

Matthew was not afraid even though Andrew approached him angrily. He looked at him and shook his head, scoffing loudly before speaking.

"Don't tell me the preacher wants to fight? Heh! Some preacher you are! You couldn't do it for her, and now that she's getting it, regularly I might add, you don't want to hear about it?

What happened to your speeches about patience, saving souls, forgiveness, love, understanding....oh and turning the other cheek? Was that all a load of crap or did God tell you to say those things? Huh? Can you even tell?"

Will Of the Flesh, Only Human

ANDREW stopped in his tracks when he heard those words. He stood still on the bottom step leading to the house as Matthew faced him and raised an eyebrow scrutinizing him suspiciously. He slowly walked down the stairs but continued to speak to Andrew.

"You were feeding that trash to your followers, but it doesn't really apply to YOU because you are better than they are, right Preacher? You are closer to God than they are, right? You are his...uh...what? Speaker? One of the examples for the others to follow...am I right? Well, aren't you?"

Matthew stopped a stair away from Andrew and scoffed. They stood there eyeing each other in silence for a few uneasy moments.

Andrew wanted to hit Matthew with all his might, but knew that God did not want him to attack this man no matter how angry he became. However, the thoughts he had continued to taunt him as badly as Matthew had done.

"Just lift one arm, swing and be done with it! Andrew! Snap out of it! This kid had sex with Cheryl...in YOUR bed! You cannot just stand there and let him gloat about it! Beat his head into his ass! Knock that smug grin off his face and watch it roll down the stairs! Just do something for goodness sake! Don't let him talk stupid and walk away!"

Andrew's thoughts echoed in his mind as he fought for control.

"Cheryl slept with him! She betrayed you! She let this boy have her body, which is supposed to be yours! She's your wife! He touched her, kissed her, made love to her in YOUR house, in YOUR bed, she turned on you for him! Do something! Do something! Don't let them have the last laugh! Get them both! Make them pay for hurting you like this!"

Andrew's thoughts were running wild with his increasing rage.

"They are making a fool out of you! You deserve better! You go to work every day to make sure that she has everything she wants, but she sleeps with this kid while you are away! She needs to suffer along with this kid! They both need to be hurt badly for what they've done to you! Hit him! Then go and beat her!"

Andrew knew hitting Cheryl was out of the question, but giving Matthew a good old-fashioned beating would have been his ultimate pleasure from the whole ordeal. He breathed deeply and closed his eyes, attempting to calm himself. He attempted to clear his mind of all the negative thoughts and ignore Matthew's taunting details about how he had sex with Cheryl on numerous occasions.

Matthew raised an eyebrow smirking slightly while he looked at Andrew as if he were challenging him to do it.

"What's the matter? Don't you have a *tongue*, preacher?"

 Matthew said in his most irritating voice. He was pretending to be concerned, but clearly mocking Andrew. He looked directly into Andrew's eyes and began to smile. Andrew frowned angrily as Matthew slowly covered his mouth as if he were surprised by Andrew's angry reaction to his words.

"Oh wow... did I hit a nerve, rev? That was below the belt wasn't it? My...uh..... Sincerest .....Apologies, sir, I forgot that you don't know how to use your tongue. How stupid of me....no, seriously, Cheryl told me. She told me many things, in between.... uh... how do I put this.....ummm....our sessions. She couldn't stop telling me how much better I am than you are in bed simply because I like to experiment and...we both know that you....do everything.... and I stress ...everything... by the book. She likes MY tongue a whoooole lot! Man! You should hear her. She absolutely loves it!"

Andrew stared at Matthew with his eyes in the top of his head. He was beyond angry. He visualized himself choking Matthew, making him cough up blood as he struggled to free himself furiously from Andrew's unbreakable grasp. He imagined Matthew's face beginning to turn blue as he choked him with all his might.

"Now, say that again, you useless boy!" Andrew said angrily to Matthew in his head as he saw himself choke Matthew lifeless. He wanted desperately to grab Matthew in his anger, but he still fought to resist the urge.

Andrew was clearly struggling with himself. He wanted to kill Matthew, but he knew he should not. God did not want him to do that. The will of his flesh was causing him to struggle like this. He took another deep breath and closed his eyes.

"Lord, help me. I'm not strong enough to do this." Andrew prayed in silence.

In reality, Matthew looked at Andrew as if he were disappointed in him himself, then he continued to walk down the stairs as he spoke.

"Well, news flash, preacher man! You aren't better than any other guy. You are only human, NOT GOD! You just hide behind that preacher stuff to try to trick yourself into thinking you are better, but we both know... you're not! You think I can't see how angry you are? THAT is just how human you really are almighty rev!"

Andrew lowered his head in shame as Matthew descended the last stair. He had done what God wanted him to do, but he didn't feel good about it at all. Matthew had bragged about stealing his wife from him directly in front of his face. He told him that he had done the things that he had refused her and she saw him more than once inside their home. Andrew had been betrayed beyond the normal betrayal. He had trusted Cheryl to do the right thing and never questioned her, but she had turned on him so quickly that he still couldn't believe it.

Matthew scoffed loudly as if he were disgusted with Andrew again, turned and walked to his car.

"Besides if you touch me, you could get trashy mouth. That wouldn't be good for your image now would it, rev? What will those blind idiots at your church think of you if you had trashy mouth?"

Matthew shook his head slowly sideways continuing his mockery.

"Tsk Tsk Tsk, shameful rev."

Andrew eyed Matthew angrily, glaring at him in silence but his fist and teeth remained clenched tightly in anger. Matthew had to add more fuel to the already roaring fire that raged inside of Andrew.

"I'm pretty sure I've been getting…. not only trashy mouth from her, but the whole sweet deal more often than you have lately too. She IS a real nice ride, after all. You've proven yourself totally worthless, to both Cheryl and to me, but it was nice meeting you anyway. I found our little chat to be rather enjoyable. We will have to do this again sometime."

Matthew tossed his head backward laughing loudly as he got into his car and drove off.

Andrew felt mortally wounded as he stood there on the stairs to his house in silence. Matthew had confirmed his worst fear and done it so boldly. Matthew acted as if he knew Andrew as well as he knew Cheryl.

Andrew felt ashamed, humiliated and angered. In her betrayal of their marriage, Cheryl had told Matthew everything about their private life. She confided in a total stranger before she brought him into their home then took him into their bed.

At first, Andrew wanted to kill Matthew for what he did, but then thought that Matthew did manage to make a point, even if he was irritating and more than worthy of punching in the face ….repeatedly.

Cheryl would never have sought him if Andrew had made her happy. This point resonated in his head as if it were a record skipping. He shook his head in an attempt to remove the thought, but it lingered still. No matter how hard he tried to think of something else, the one thought he did not want to face continued to haunt him.

"Cheryl would never have done this if I had pleased her when she asked me to."

He felt his heart aching inside his chest as his anger subsided and his misery, imagining his wife in the arms of Matthew began to grow.

He thought of her laughing and smiling happily as they danced from the times before they argued. She was happy then and he could not bring those days back to her. Then his thoughts slowly changed and he saw the two of them lying in his bed naked laughing at him. He was hurt beyond reason. He had devoted his life to Cheryl and she betrayed him so easily. His pride, heart and very soul were all wounded, but he still wanted her. He was sure that he still wanted her, until yet another thought occurred to him.

"She doesn't think I'm a man?" He thought as he remembered Matthew's words.

"She thinks I'm man enough, apparently more of a man than you..."

Andrew heard Matthew's words playing repeatedly in his mind.

He closed his eyes, lowered his head and stood there on the steps in front of the house that he and Cheryl had decided was the perfect place to call home together.

He wished he could go back to that moment in their life and start over from there. He felt that he had failed her and knew she was not happy with being married to him.

He believed she deserved better and decided that if she wanted better, he would allow her to have it.

Letting Go

"**SOMETIMES** letting go isn't easy for anyone, but if it's God's will, it shall be done."

Andrew told himself as he slowly dragged himself into the house that he once called home. Now he thought of it as a brothel where sinful acts were committed. It was no longer a sacred place and could no longer provide sanctuary for him. Cheryl had defiled it with Matthew and now he knew all about it.

Andrew thought about confronting her to tell her what Matthew had confessed, but decided that he would be too angry to talk to her calmly. He needed to vent his anger in another way and decided to work out. He went to his weight training room in the basement and worked out there, unable to focus on his routine, but clearly imagining Cheryl in bed with Matthew in spite of his reluctance to do so intentionally.

"Stupid punk kid! I should have…" His voice was practically an angry growl, but he stopped himself from finishing his sentence. Then he quickly changed it to something better.

"God's will was done as it shall always be. Thank God that I didn't do anything he did not want me to do. Blessed be the name of The Lord."

Andrew took a few deep breaths in attempt to soothe himself. He knew he would find no human comfort from anyone else, especially Cheryl, who he had always needed the most.

He knew that anger was not going to solve the problem that he had begun with his rejection of Cheryl. He decided that it was his fault because she came to him first to tell him what she wanted from him sexually, but he would not comply with her no matter how she pleaded with him about it. She even tried to explain to him that it was right to please his wife, but he would not budge from his opinion. He shook his head and walked away from her, leaving her standing there, trying to figure out what to do next. He was very inconsiderate to her, so her turning to Matthew was almost justified, even if he was a punk kid.

Of course he didn't realize it at the time, but talking to Matthew made him take notice in the error of his ways.

He should have pleased her. He should have been more understanding and attentive to her. He should not have just rejected her. He should not have made her feel alone and unloved because of how she felt. Marriage was more than just sex, it's listening, comforting, nurturing, protecting, and learning from each other.

Andrew had turned Cheryl away just because of the sex issue. He closed his eyes and took another deep breath. He was truly sorry for making her feel abandoned and rejected. He suddenly realized he had practically handed his wife over to Matthew on a silver platter.

Andrew could no longer lift his weights. He sat on his bench catching his breath, staring at the wall in front of him. Then he looked at the door.

"What have I done? I know what I've done. I've chased her away from me. I made things easy for any man to have taken her away from me. She must have felt so ashamed, ugly and unloved. I was so stupid. I should have made it clear to her then but...Now she's spending more time with that punk than me."

Andrew was emotionally defeated now. He shook his head in disgust with himself as he slowly made his way to the guest room. He wanted peace, but he knew he would not have that for a long time now. Peace was as distant to him as Heaven itself. He felt as if he were carrying his weights on his back, but there was nothing there. His body was simply heavy with all the guilt, blame, and shame of what he had just learned. He wondered if he could ever relieve himself of these emotions, but also believed that he deserved to feel them. He was not the man everyone who looked up to him thought him to be. Now, he was nothing.

As Andrew showered, he thought about Cheryl again. He didn't want to make her miserable. He hadn't meant to make her feel rejected or to push her into the arms of another man, but there was nothing he could do about that. It had happened, according the Matthew, it happened several times. Andrew could not handle the thought of another man with his wife, if God weren't present in his life. He knew that God would get him through this and help him to get on with his life even though things seemed bleak. "God is the worker of many miracles and He will see me through this situation too. I know He will. I must be patient, and trust Him. HE is the mighty conqueror of all things."

Andrew got out of the shower, slipped into some pajama pants and got into bed, slowly. He was emotionally and physically drained and needed rest desperately, but as he tried to sleep Matthew's words kept coming back to him.

"I've been here a few times before…"

Andrew could no longer stand it now. He clenched his fists and teeth together tightly in anger and frustration. He could no longer sleep in this bed, or any bed in the house now. Andrew jumped out of bed and got dressed as quickly as he could.

Andrew could no longer stay here and headed back toward the front door. He no longer wanted to live there in the house that he used to call home. His wife's betrayal had rendered the house useless to him now. He could never return here because the home was full of memories, good and bad. He packed a bag of his belongings quickly, flung the guest room door open and made his way down the stairs toward the door as quickly as he could. He didn't care if Cheryl had heard him or not now, but much to his relief, she did not open the door to the bedroom as he left the house. He didn't think he could handle looking at her right now anyway.

 He hurried down the stairs, tossed his bag into the backseat as he took his place behind the steering wheel of his truck and started it up. He looked at the house once more as the emotions began to build up inside of him again.

"All those years…… Why? Why Cheryl? Why did you destroy everything we once had? What's more important is was it really worth all this?"

He rubbed his temples as if he had a massive headache, but the pain he felt really came from his heart. Cheryl was the love of his life and she had hurt him worse than anyone had ever hurt him before. He wanted her to stop him from leaving, but she didn't even come to the door, or window. She clearly did not care whether he left or stayed.

Andrew shook his head in disappointment then anger as he shifted the gear of his truck then drove to a motel where he got a room for the night even though he could not sleep at all. He spent the night looking at the ceiling in his motel room. He had left the house without even checking to see if Cheryl was alive. His anger would not allow him to look in on her.

The next morning came and Andrew went to work as usual. He did not want to talk about his marital problems with his co-workers, but during his break, he called a few attorneys to discuss his options. He wanted to know more about divorce proceedings and everything involved. He also consulted his Bible for some answers to questions. He was very distracted at work that day because he had to make a decision and he knew he would have to make it soon.

Andrew wondered what life would be like without Cheryl. He knew he would be miserable without her, but she was miserable with him. He wondered if there was anything, he could do to both forgive her betrayal of their sacred union and to make her happy in the future. He shook his head believing it to be hopeless.

"I will be miserable, but I would rather be miserable than to continue to make her miserable." He thought.

Andrew had made his decision. He rubbed his eyes, then made his way to the privacy of his office where he picked up the telephone and began to dial an attorney.

"Hello, my name is Andrew Montgomery. I am seeking legal advice to file for a divorce from my wife of five years, Cheryl."

 **About the Author**

Tyler is not only a writer, she also edits, creates videos for novels and is the current Editor-In-Chief for the magazine, *For the People, By the People.*

In her spare time Tyler loves to spend time with her family.

Christian Carnal Cravings

❖ Why do you think it was so hard for both Cheryl and Rachel to discuss their problems?

❖ Do you think Andrew was a good husband?

❖ What are your views on sex in a marriage? Are their restrictions?

❖ What are your views on sex/masturbation for singles?

❖ Do you think Matthew cared for Cheryl? Why or Why not?

❖ Do you feel Sean cared for Rachel? Why or Why not?

❖ What are some things you think Cheryl could have done differently?

❖ What are some things you think Rachel could have done differently?

❖ Why do you think Rachel found it hard to talk to her sister when she said her sister was 'wild'?

❖ Can you relate to either woman? If so, in what manner?

The controversy and drama in the lives of Rachel Jansen and Cheryl Montgomery doesn't end here ...

Christian Carnal Cravings:
The Saga Continues

By Tyler

Coming Summer 2015

Forbidden Pleasure

RACHEL unlocked her car door, placed the folders beneath the passenger seat, and then locked the door before shutting it. She had parked her car in the company parking lot, so she thought it was safe there. She hadn't bothered to question the safety of her vehicle before, however, her conversation with Faye made her begin to worry.

"What if she has friends that are security guards here? She could total my car and get away with it. That wouldn't be nice." Rachel's thoughts began to unnerve her. She looked around and spotted a security guard walking slowly through the parking lot. He was making the rounds which they did on a regular basis. Most of the attorneys had rich expensive luxury cars so they wanted them to be guarded like gold in the parking lot. Rachel didn't want anything so materialistic, so she bought a car that she believed was reliable and was proud of it. As long as her car got her where she needed to go safely, she was fine. She wasn't into buying show cars.

"God is protecting my car, so I know that nothing will happen, but if it does, God has something better in store for me, so I'm not going to stress over such a silly thing."

Rachel managed to calm herself easily this time. She was impressed with herself even though this victory over her mind was nothing in comparison to the incidents at the nightclub. She still felt proud of herself and could not help but thank God for her new attitude even if it were only a minor thing. She knew she would definitely need to be positive when she saw Cheryl again. She exited the parking lot and headed toward the building.

Rachel held her cell phone tightly as she thought about calling Frances, then ultimately decided not to because she didn't want to anger her further. She had already decided to let Frances vent until she was calm enough to talk to her and initiate the contact between them. She wasn't focusing on anything at the moment. She simply missed talking to her sister, until she bumped into something that was solid.

Rachel stepped back and shook her head as she composed herself. Then she heard a familiar voice.

"Oh, I'm sorry, I was looking for….Rachel?"

Rachel quickly looked up and recognized Reverend Andrew Montgomery.

"Oh my! Reverend." Rachel was surprised to see him here. She was taken completely off guard by his presence and spoke without thinking.

"I thought I bumped into a wall. You are so solid! Wow!" Rachel gasped then covered her mouth in surprise as the words escaped her mouth before she knew it.

Andrew smiled, scoffing slightly.

"Well, I hope I didn't hurt you. Are you sure you are okay?" Andrew touched her shoulder gently as he questioned her.

Rachel eyed Andrew curiously. He was wearing his work uniform, not the usual dress suit. He wore jeans, construction boots and a tee shirt beneath his short sleeved unbuttoned work shirt. Rachel couldn't take her eyes off his torso. When she bumped into him, she felt like she had run into a wall because his body was that firm.

"Oh wow!" Rachel thought as she bit her lip unable to tear her eyes away from his body.

Rachel hadn't thought of Andrew as an attractive man before, but now after having bumped into him, she began to look at him differently. She didn't mean to, but the thoughts just came to her in spite of part of her brain telling her not to think like that. Rachel touched her forehead and looked at her feet. She didn't want to make eye contact with Andrew now that the impure thoughts were forcing their way into her mind. She wondered what he must think of her now.

"Rachel? Are you okay?" Andrew asked again.

"Yes. Thank you I'm fine. I wasn't watching were I was going. You see, Frances and I had an argument and I...well, I have been distracted. I miss her." Rachel said sadly.

Andrew began to look sad as well. He too had missed someone greatly. He didn't want to talk about that at this moment though. He mustered up his most pleasant facial expression as he slowly offered advice and encouraging words to Rachel, but really spoke them for himself.

"I know what it's like to miss someone that you usually share everything with. It's not a good feeling, but when that does happen, we just need to remember that God is always with us. His love is greater than any human love and he will never let us down."

Andrew knew he needed to hear those words for himself while he spoke. He nodded slightly and blinked then turned his head toward the building. He did not look at Rachel for few moments as he thought about Cheryl. He focused on the address written on the paper again to avoid revealing the sadness in his face.

The both of them stood there on the sidewalk in front of the building in silence. Andrew looked up at the numbers on the building, as Rachel slowly looked at him. The woman in her wanted to hold him tightly, but she knew better than to do that. She couldn't help thinking lustfully of Andrew now that he had displayed his vulnerable human side. She instantly found him attractive in spite of everything she already knew.

"He is such a kind man and … very… handsome!" Rachel thought as she stared at him.

"Cheryl is very very lucky…." She thought until she remembered that Cheryl had cheated on him and he was filing for a divorce. Rachel could not help but think of how she would treat Andrew if she were married to him. She didn't want to judge Cheryl intentionally, but she began to question her sanity.

 Rachel did not want to tell him anything that he didn't already know even if she had stumbled upon the last bit of information. She had seen them together in church on so many occasions; she was saddened to learn what was happening with them. She wasn't the only one who believed that they were the perfect couple. The entire congregation looked up to the couple and even deemed them as living blueprints for successful marriages.

Andrew turned his eyes away from the building and looked at a small piece of paper with a hand written address on it.

"I thought this was the place, but it's not. I must apologize again for almost knocking you down. It was an accident, but it is very nice to see you, Rachel. I was trying to find the address to this building, but I didn't mean to hurt anyone in the process." Andrew tried to laugh as he spoke to her making it sound like a joke, but he wasn't in the mood to laugh.

Rachel smiled politely.

"I'm not hurt so it's fine, Reverend. I just … well … was taken off guard, that's all. It is nice to bump into you though." Rachel spoke softly.

She looked at Andrew as if he were another man and not the reverend of her church. She immediately noticed that he seemed out of place here in the downtown area. He looked at the buildings as he tried to figure out which way he should go.

"I can help if you are lost, that is if you would like me to help." Rachel offered.

"I thank you, Rachel. I don't come to the downtown area very often, but I guess I should start doing this. I get lost if I'm not in a familiar place. Cheryl always said…" Andrew quickly stopped speaking. He didn't want to talk about Cheryl now.

Rachel picked up on the mention of Cheryl immediately and helped to move the conversation forward.

"I spoke to her yesterday. She came to my apartment and we had a nice conversation. She helped me to feel better about things that were weighing me down in my life. I like to think that maybe she learned a little from our talk as well. I don't know what I would have done without her help…or yours. You both have been just great to me. I think you both are very inspiring."

Rachel stared at Andrew as she spoke for a moment. She noticed that he had grown both silent and sad. "Is everything okay?" she asked innocently pretending not to know what was wrong. Deep down, she felt awful for him and Cheryl too.

"Well, I am not sure about that Rachel. I've been confused about a great deal of things and I need to really concentrate on God for a while. I'm glad Cheryl was able to help you out though. That's a wonderful blessing. She is a very special woman."

Andrew paused, looked at the written address once more, and then continued to speak to Rachel.

"I don't really want to be a bother to you, but if you could just tell me the way to go so that I could find this address." He said as he showed her the piece of paper. "I'll be on my way. You work this way don't you?" Andrew asked as Rachel looked at the paper.

"I work right here in this building for Waters, Anthony and Mitchell, Inc. Attorneys at Law." Rachel smiled as she pointed to the building they were stationed in front of. Andrew shook his head.

"Now that is embarrassing. I practically knocked you down in front of your own place of employment. I feel another apology is necessary here." Andrew rubbed his forehead now and slowly smiled. Rachel smiled. She thought the gesture was cute.

"Apology accepted, Reverend." Rachel extended her hand and shook his. Andrew laughed softly.

"That's nice of you Rachel. I do appreciate your forgiveness, but please call me Andrew." Andrew smiled while speaking to her.

Rachel decided to help him and return to work before she said something way out of control and flirtatious unintentionally.

"The building that you are in search of is straight down this way. Just stay on this side of the street and keep going. It's a really large building. You can't miss it. I know where it is, in fact, I just left there. I could show you where it is if you like."

Rachel didn't want Andrew to get lost, so she made the offer but Andrew didn't want any company tagging along for what he was about to do. He had to get used to being alone so now was as good a time as any to start. He shook his head as he spoke.

"Thank you again, Rachel but I think I can handle it from here though. I do appreciate all your help. It would probably be best if you got back to work, before they fire you for helping a truly lost soul out." Andrew took the piece of paper as Rachel returned it to him.

"You are more than welcome, Reverend...."

"Please, call me Andrew. It isn't fair for me to call you only Rachel when you are an attorney. Besides, first names are more informal and much easier to say, so no more formalities. Call me Andrew and I will call you Rachel, just to save us time during or next conversation, especially if I almost knock you down again. Have a blessed evening Rachel" Andrew smiled as he turned and slowly began to walk away.

Rachel smiled, then replied. "You too, re... I mean, Andrew!" She quickly stopped herself from calling him reverend again just as he had requested.

She headed back to her office but decided to turn around. Andrew was standing there. He had been watching her walk away from him. Rachel smiled nervously and waved. He waved back and Rachel watched him disappear into the crowd.

She felt a familiar tingle between her legs and it shocked her. "What kind of woman am I to feel what I'm feeling for my friend's husband?"

_____*CCC2*_____

A Cursed Miracle

CHERYL left Rachel's apartment feeling a little better about things even though she knew talking to Andrew about what was going on would be difficult. She knew it would be the most difficult thing she had ever done. Telling him about her infidelity with Matthew was a conversation that she dreaded immensely. She shook her head in regret as she tried to think of what to say.

"Honey, I....not good. Maybe I should say...Andrew, I have to tell you something... sure! Great! That's gonna work a miracle!" Cheryl was disappointed with herself. The more she thought about it, the less she wanted to do it.

"Well, I don't have a choice now. I messed things up, so I have to do my best to fix them now." Cheryl scolded herself sharply. She took another deep breath and attempted to relax.

 She drove along the path leading to the house and parked her car in the two-car garage. She took a moment to breathe as she stared at the house and allowed the memories to unfold inside her head. She had been so happy living there with Andrew. He had always taken very good care of her even before they were married. He bought her everything she wanted.

She knew he could not afford some of the things she asked for, but he found a way to get whatever she asked for always. He borrowed money from his parents and got a job in a department store as a stocking clerk in addition to working for his father on weekends while in school to help pay for the things she wanted. He didn't mind working to make sure she had what she wanted because he told her on several occasions that he thought she was more than worth spoiling. She was always the first to admit that he spoiled her rotten, but she was happy that he did. Then she began to think that maybe spoiling her wasn't such a good idea because when she didn't get her way, she gave him pure hell. This was definitely one of those times. Andrew would be going through hell because of her spoiled nature again.

Cheryl wished that she had never met Matthew now. He was nothing like Andrew was to her. Matthew was very last minute, spontaneous and wild. She had craved that, well, she thought she did before, but now she would give anything to be free of Matthew for good. He only bought her one gift, the lingerie he told her that he wanted to see her wear when they first met.

Andrew bought her gifts almost every day. He bought flowers, jewelry, tickets to exotic locations and events that she said she wanted to attend. He bought her everything he knew she would like and she loved them all. He even knew how to buy fancy dresses for her. He loved seeing her try on the things he bought for her, at least, he told her as much.

Cheryl snapped out of her happy thoughts of times with Andrew abruptly. She told herself that she had to tell Andrew before Matthew did. She exited her car and began to make her way to the house slowly, trudging along as if her legs were too heavy to lift until she remembered the answering machine and began to climb the stairs to the house as quickly as she could.

Once inside, she rushed to the telephone to check messages, but to her surprise there weren't any new messages recorded. She thought that was strange, but then she thought Andrew had listened to them all which gave her a sense of unease. She didn't know if Matthew had left a message or not. Her worry began to grow into a panic and picked up the phone immediately dialing Andrew's work number as rapidly as her fingers would move across the telephone.

"New Foundations Construction Company, how may I help you?" said the secretary.

"Oh, hello Teresa this is Mrs. Montgomery. Is my husband available?" Cheryl spoke calmly and waited for Teresa's reply even though she was still in panic mode.

"Oh, I'm sorry Mrs. Montgomery. I didn't recognize your voice. You just missed him. He said he had some business to take care of and he was leaving work early, so he's gone for the day." Teresa replied. Cheryl was confused now.

"He did? Did he say anything else?" Cheryl was trying to find out why Andrew left early, but didn't want to appear too anxious. She was pretty sure that she was failing at this though.

"No, he just said he had some business to take care of." Teresa responded.

Cheryl began to feel disappointed now. She had wanted to talk to him, but now she wouldn't be able to let him know that she wanted to talk. She decided to try his cell phone, but if he were driving, she knew he would not answer. It was not in his routine to talk on the phone while he drove. He said it was illegal, so he never did it.

"Okay, thank you Teresa. I'll try his cell phone."

"Oh, you won't be able to reach him that way either. He left his cell phone. He said he didn't need it for a while and left it here. He told me that he was locking his desk, but he meant to leave his cell phone. He didn't want to be interrupted while he took care of things. I thought it was very peculiar, but he's the boss, so I didn't question." Teresa covered her mouth. She had forgotten that she was talking to the boss's wife.

"I'm sorry Mrs..." Teresa began, but Cheryl interrupted.

"It's okay. That was very strange of him. In fact, that wasn't like him at all, but thank you Teresa. I do appreciate the information. If he should return before I can reach him, please ask him to call home."

"Of course, Mrs. Montgomery I will definitely do that. Good bye." Teresa hung up the phone.

Cheryl was frozen with fear. She couldn't move a muscle. She stood there in silence grasping the telephone receiver tightly as she struggled to breathe. The dial tone buzzed in her ear causing her to start, gaze at it strangely, and then slowly lower the receiver to the base. She wondered where he was going and why he was leaving his cell phone at the office.

"Maybe he's coming here to try to make things right between us."

Cheryl thought this was farfetched, but she needed something positive to hold onto. Once she had said it to herself enough, she began to grow excited about it. She rushed to the kitchen and quickly decided what to make for dinner. She began to cook his favorite, pot roast and mashed potatoes with gravy, then rushed up the stairs. She wanted to look her best for Andrew's arrival. She showered quickly, then slipped into one of her sexy dresses that she knew Andrew loved to see her wear. It was one of the dresses that he had bought for her one night they were hosting a dinner party.

It was a dark blue velvet strapless dress. The dress hem delicately grazed her ankles in the front and slightly trailed in back. She had not worn it to the party because she thought it was too dressy, but she knew he loved seeing her in it so she wore it when she dressed up for private dinner parties with him. She put on her diamond openwork choker with circular and old-cut diamond fringe and floral motifs.

The necklace was her most expensive gift from him. It cost him well over $200,000 dollars and he took out a loan to purchase it when they were in school. He paid it off when he became an engineer though, so he was proud of this accomplishment. She took extra special care of it in return. She wore it on her wedding day but for the most part, she kept it locked away in her wall safe. She loved the necklace, but she would gladly give it away for Andrew's forgiveness.

She applied makeup then rushed to check on the dinner. Everything was perfect, so she decided to set the table. She placed the best Mongolian fine china on the table. She set silk roses in the vase then stepped back to take an observatory look. Once she was satisfied with the table, she rushed to a mirror and checked her appearance again.

"This should be okay. I don't look too bad." She told herself.

She walked to the kitchen to check the food when she heard a car approaching, so she made her way to the table. She began to feel nervous now and tried to think of what to say to start the conversation, but in her panic, she couldn't. She decided to let him begin. She just wanted to hold him in her arms and beg him to forgive her.

After a few minutes of waiting in a near panic, she didn't hear anything else, so she walked to the door and peeked outside. The car was driving away down the path back to the street. She initially wanted to call out, but stopped herself when she realized that she had not recognized the car.

"That isn't Andrew's truck. Who was that? Where is Andrew?" Cheryl thought.

She looked in the mailbox, collected it quickly then returned to the inside of the house.

Cheryl had been sitting at the dining room table waiting for Andrew for hours now. She didn't know what was taking him so long to get there. She rose from her chair and walked to the door. He was not there. The sun had gone down and she felt her good spirits disappearing with the increasing darkness.

Cheryl had been waiting for Andrew's arrival for nearly three hours. She rose from her seat at the dining room table and went into the kitchen. She opened the wine cabinet and removed a bottle blinking hard to keep the tears from falling onto her face. She opened it and began to drink. She had lost all hope now and told herself that Andrew was not coming home. She kicked off her shoes blue velvet stilettos, walked to the living room and sat on the couch with the bottle in her hand. She was very disappointed now and needed to vent desperately. She closed her eyes as her anger began to take control.

"Slut! That's what I am. I'm a slut! I'm not worth fighting for or even thinking about. Why did I think he was actually going to come back to me? Why would he do something that stupid? Andrew is not an idiot! I am!" Cheryl took another long drink from the wine bottle, wiped her mouth with the back of her hand roughly, and then scoffed loudly before speaking.

"Yeah right! Why would a decent man like Andrew want a whore like me for a wife? He deserves someone…. like Rachel, not me. She's a good girl, she would make him happy. That's for sure. She'd probably even give him the children he wanted. I'm just so useless! What did he ever see in me? He was blind when he married me. He should have run the other way." Cheryl continued drinking allowing the alcohol to add to her anguish. She thought it would soothe her, but instead it increased her brewing rage.

 She didn't care about how she felt anymore or what she said. She convinced herself that she felt better for now and that was fine with her.

Cheryl tossed the empty wine bottle at the dining room table, striking the flower arrangement in the middle. The vase shattered upon impact and the bits of glass clinked atop the dishes. Cheryl walked slowly to the table and stared at it.

"Andrew bought me these lovely plates and glasses. I told him that I wanted them, and he made sure that I got them. He was always so sweet to me. I don't deserve him. I don't deserve him at all. I don't deserve this house, these clothes, this necklace, these dishes; I don't deserve anything he gave me. All I ever gave him was pain and suffering. Why did he choose me?" Cheryl spoke as the tears began to fall down her cheeks.

Cheryl frowned as the rage she felt grew. She didn't deserve her pretty gifts that Andrew bought for her. She screamed loudly as she began to slide her hands across the table, knocking dishes to the floor repeatedly. She rushed to the china cabinet, flung the doors open and began to hurl the dishes, glasses and other decorations displayed there, into the walls angrily.

"Stupid! Stupid! Stupid!" she shouted in anger.

Cheryl continued to destroy the delicate trinkets in her fit of rage. When she was done with everything in the china cabinet, she threw pots, pans, skillets, anything she could get her hands on into the walls. She no longer cared for such things. She used to be proud of her house, but now, it was nothing to her. She hated it! She hated being there and she hated herself the most.

All of a sudden she was overcome with nausea like she'd never experienced before. She ran to the bathroom and threw up but it was only dry heaves because she hadn't eaten since earlier the day before at Rachel's house. She reached under the sink to grab some mouthwash and noticed her unopened box of tampons. She'd bought them several weeks ago in preparation for her period that was always on time – like clockwork. Until now.

Cheryl realized she was more than three weeks late! What was happening? But the doctors said ... she couldn't possibly be ... Could it be true? She didn't know whether to be happy or devastated. IF she was pregnant – who was her child's father? Andrew or Matthew?

_____CCC2_____

Tyler Books Inc

*"Unlocking Universal Doors
through Literary Services"*

HTTP://TYLERBOOKS2014.WIX.COM/MONICA

The Butterfly Typeface Publishing

"We make good great!"

WWW.THEBUTTERFLYTYPEFACE.COM

www.ingramcontent.com/pod-product-compliance
Lightning Source LLC
Chambersburg PA
CBHW080820020726
47501CB00009B/2358